Nathalia Buttface

NIGEL SMITH has been a journalist, busker, TV comedy producer and script writer, winning an award for his BBC 4 radio comedy, *Vent,* based on his own life-threatening brain illness. More importantly, he has been – and still is – an embarrassing dad. Much like Nathalia Buttface, his three children are continually mortified by his ill-advised trousers, comedic hats, low-quality jokes, poorly chosen motor vehicles, unique sense of direction and unfortunate ukulele playing. Unlike his hero, Ivor Bumolé, he doesn't write Christmas cracker jokes for a living. Yet.

First published in Great Britain by HarperCollins *Children's Books* in 2014
HarperCollins *Children's Books* is a division of HarperCollins*Publishers* Ltd,
77–85 Fulham Palace Road, Hammersmith, London W6 8JB

Visit us on the web at
www.harpercollinschildrensbooks.co.uk

1

Nathalia Buttface and the Most Embarrassing
Dad in the World
Text © Nigel Smith 2014
Illustrations © Sarah Horne 2014

Nigel Smith and Sarah Horne assert the moral right
to be identified as the author and illustrator of this work.

ISBN 978-0-00-754521-6

CRINGE!

MIX
Paper from
responsible sources
FSC
www.fsc.org
FSC C007454

FSC™ is a non-profit international organisation established to promote
the responsible management of the world's forests. Products carrying the
FSC label are independently certified to assure consumers that they come
from forests that are managed to meet the social, economic and
ecological needs of present and future generations,
and other controlled sources.

Find out more about HarperCollins and the environment at
www.harpercollins.co.uk/green

To my children, Tara Jayne Cushion, Jamesy Wambles and Binky Boo Poo-shoes. Who know that what really happened was far, far worse.

CHAPTER ONE

····

THE MOST EMBARRASSING DAD IN THE WORLD WAS embarrassing Nathalia even before she was born.

He went and married Mum, didn't he? So when baby Nat was born, she ended up with Dad's last name instead of Mum's. Mum's last name was De Montfort. A very ladylike name, with just a whiff of the exotic. Nathalia De Montfort was a name to be reckoned with.

I could be Prime Minister with that name, she would think, daydreaming, *or a supermodel. I could be a flying vet, or a singing brain surgeon. I could win two Nobel prizes – one for making things go bang and one for stopping things going bang.* Nathalia De Montfort could win three Michelin stars, four Oscars and a grand prix in the same weekend. *She* could be the first eleven-year-old girl on Mars.

Thanks to Dad she wasn't Nathalia De Montfort.

She was Nathalia Bumolé.

"It's pronounced *Bew-mow–lay*," Dad would tell her patiently, time and time again. "If anyone says differently, the joke's on them."

"On *them*? The joke's on THEM? That's not how it works, Dad. The joke will definitely NOT be on them. It will be massively on me. It was massively on me all through my last school, and it will be massively on me in this one too."

But her words were lost over the crunching of gears and the shouty morning DJ, who was called Cabbage.

"It's back to school day," burbled the fathead,

as if the millions of sulky kids now being dragged sleepily out of their beds didn't know. "So step away from your Easter eggs and get ready for the great summer term. Which means rain, exams, sports days and asthma attacks. Ha ha ha."

Then he and his witless companions roared with laughter. *Great, summer term, thanks for reminding me*, thought Nathalia, scratchy in her new school blazer. *And I'm the only kid IN THE WORLD starting at a new school today. I'll have to walk into a class full of people who all know each other. And they'll ALL stare at me.*

"Do you know how embarrassing that is, Dad?" Nat shouted.

But Dad wasn't listening. He was still wittering on about her stupid name.

"…and it's a very old name."

Well that's all right then, she thought sourly. *If it's* old. She sighed. Dad thought anything old was good, even though it might plainly be rubbish – old houses, old music, Nathalia's nan.

And especially the mega-rubbish old camper

van she was currently being carted around in. She sank lower into the van's cloth sofa as she glimpsed a couple of kids in the distinctive purple and blue uniform of her new school.

The van had a name. Of course it did. Only The Most Embarrassing Dad In The World would give a noisy, rusty, smoky machine a name. He called it Ned The Atomic Dustbin. Nathalia thought that was stupid. For a start, it ran on petrol not nuclear fusion, so it wasn't atomic at all. She had to admit, however, it WAS a dustbin.

"It's a skip with wheels," said Mum one day, refusing a lift to the train station. "If I was seen in that, my company would lose a hundred points on the stock exchange overnight."

Nathalia wasn't sure what that meant but she liked it when Mum talked business. And she especially liked it when Dad got told off too.

Looking at her watch again, Nat told herself she wasn't nervous about her new school. She had thought hard about it and now she had school sussed. She knew it wasn't about being popular.

She wanted to be NOT UNPOPULAR. At her old school, most of the time she'd have liked to hide in a cardboard box at the back of the class but a girl called Amy Chan had got to the box first. Amy Chan was definitely NOT popular.

Nat had found it hard to make friends and she mostly blamed Dad. He was always embarrassing her.

For example, he always gave her such rubbish advice. At primary school he kept telling her to 'join in a bit more'. One day her classmates were talking about their imaginary friends. Nat hadn't got one but decided to listen to his advice and 'join in'. On the spot she invented an imaginary friend called Jenny Jennifer. Jenny Jennifer, she said, had a white face, long white hair and long white fingernails, and lived on a fairground ride. Noticing everyone had gone quiet, Nat warmed to her story. Jenny Jennifer sang nursery rhymes backwards, could only be seen when the carousel went round too quickly and – here Nat went for the sympathy vote – only appeared to children who were sad.

Three girls ran off screaming before Nat realised she'd invented less of an imaginary friend and more of an EVIL TERRIFYING GHOST.

Stupid Dad advice.

And now she was starting at her *second* secondary school in a year. They'd had to move so that Mum could have an easier commute to her big new job. Even this was Dad's fault really. If he had a PROPER job like other dads, they could have stayed put. Nat hadn't made any friends at her last school, but to be fair she had only been there a few months, and anyway she was sure she had been just about to. One girl had even said 'hello'. Now she would have to start all over again.

And so far it was a TERRIBLE start. She'd got up late because Dad hadn't forced her to get up earlier like a proper dad would have done. And now she was being driven to school in this *contraption*, surrounded by… surrounded by…

Hang on, she thought, *what IS all this junk*

I'm surrounded by?

Newspapers, crates, wires, pots, pans, lightbulbs, magazines, half-empty toolboxes, reels of fuse wire, two burst spacehoppers, a bike with only one wheel that was supposed to have two wheels, a bike with no wheels that was supposed to have one wheel, a ukulele, six unwieldy old computer hard drives with less processing power than Mum's new hairdryer, a croquet set, a blackboard, a whiteboard, fifteen full black plastic bags, a garden chair, a garden bench, a garden gnome, shoes, a candle in a wine bottle, a motorbike engine, four boxes of LPs called things like *The Strobing Bogeys, live at Preston Civic Centre*, a broken record player, a huge kicked-in speaker with Mum's footprint still just visible, a box of yellowed paperbacks with either spaceships, dragons, or tanks on, a box of yellowed paperbacks with spaceships, dragons AND tanks on, postcards, rubber masks, and various wooden objects that could only be described as 'objects, wooden, various.'

Nathalia HATED the van. And she hated gobbling her breakfast cereal at the little table in the back of the van due to them being late. As she shoved the Dog's shaggy – and, she noticed, uncomfortably – *milky* head away from her bowl, Nat tried to get comfy between a box of Scalextric parts and a filing cabinet.

She stared at her reflection in the grimy window, suddenly wishing she had a lemony-scented window cloth. This van really was disgusting.

Her large brown eyes stared back at her. Brown eyes. She sighed; who has blonde hair and BROWN eyes? People always made a fuss about it. Grannies in caffs were the worst for fussing. *Urgh, getting kissed by whiskery old women... I'll get a rash from all the bristles*, she thought.

That was Dad's fault too. They were *his* eyes.

"Hold tight," said Dad, just after he braked violently. He'd spotted someone he knew. Even though they'd only moved here five minutes ago, he already knew EVERYONE.

Nathalia sighed as she dragged herself back out from where she was thrown under the table. She sighed as her blazer got tangled in a string of broken Christmas lights. She sighed for the *third* time when she saw the Dog wearing her cereal bowl like a soldier's hat. The Dog licked her face and his breath smelled of doggy victory.

Dad was now hanging out of the van window, chatting to a young man with a silly moustache, super-skinny trousers and a hat shaped like an upside-down bucket. *Typical Dad*, she thought. *He loves talking to young people because he thinks he's still young and cool, even though he's obviously really old. It's just so EMBARRASSING.*

She slid further down out of sight as Dad started telling the young man about how it was her first day at school and how it was a shame that she was really shy. *I'm shy NOW, you idiot*, she thought. Didn't Dad know by now that that was literally the WORST thing he could say? And she just knew he was going to say it to EVERYONE at the school gates too. She felt sick.

That's it, she decided, as he finally drove off. *No one at my new school must EVER meet Dad. At the next set of traffic lights I'm opening the slidy door and jumping out. I'm running to school and if he follows I'm just going to shout: "Help, there's a strange man following me, call the police." Maybe*, she thought, *Dad would be just put in prison long enough for me to get my GCSEs out of the way. And perhaps make just a COUPLE of friends. I'd visit him. Probably at night when no one could see, but I would visit him.*

"Nearly there!" called Dad, oblivious to the evil Nat-sized plot taking shape behind him. "Traffic's a bit bad and for some reason we seem to be late."

Right, thought Nathalia, hand poised on the slidy door lever. *There's a set of lights coming up. They're always on red. Mum says the council does it on purpose because they're communists out to stop people going about their business in very fast little cars like hers. Which is what she also says every time she gets a speeding ticket.*

Nathalia felt the van slow. *Sorry, Dad,* she thought, *but prison's quite nice these days. Nan says it's like a holiday camp...*

Nat gripped the door handle, ready to fling it open. But then...

"Brace yourself," Dad shouted, "I'm going to take a back double."

Nathalia's blood froze. There were few more terrifying words in the English language than Dad saying, "I'm going to take a back double."

Previous 'back doubles' over the years had landed them in a park, a shopping centre, an airport runway, a railway line, and, memorably, IN ANOTHER COUNTRY ENTIRELY.

Nat's knuckles were white on the handle. She had to get out. NOW. This school was going to be different. The first day was crucial – it determined the rest of your life...

CHAPTER TWO

• • • •

HALF AN HOUR LATER...

NATHALIA REALISED THAT IF TODAY WAS ANYTHING to go by, the rest of her life was going to be pretty flipping awful.

She was now unspeakably late for school. She was clinging to the branches of a conker tree. Dad was also in the tree, but of course he was dressed as a clown. Beneath them, a wild creature wreathed in smoke hissed furiously.

"I've had better Mondays, Dad," Nathalia shouted.

"At least it won't get any worse."

And then the local TV helicopter swooped overhead. A long camera lens stuck out at her, like a tongue.

"It just got ever so much worse. Stop waving your arms about, you're attracting attention."

"What's that, love?" shouted the clown. The clown who, a few minutes ago, *had been Dad*. "Sorry, I'm still trying to get a signal on this phone. I might have half a bar if I stand on tiptoe. I can't hear you over the noise of the news helicopter."

Dad the clown waved at the chopper. "Wonder what they're doing here?"

The Most Embarrassing Dad in the World waved his mobile phone above the treetop. His orange curly wig was pulled halfway over his face, his red plastic nose had come off during their mad scramble to safety, and his ballooning yellow check trousers were hanging frighteningly

low, and were ripped to bits. A string of brightly coloured hankies spilled out of his back pocket.

The news footage from this incident was later voted second in a viewers' poll of 'funniest news stories of the year', only beaten by the monkey shoving a banana in a weather girl's ear (and the monkey only won because Nat voted for it 156 times to make sure SHE didn't win).

Dad shifted his weight a little. His branch didn't look too secure. Nathalia wished she had a great big axe. She covered her face so it wouldn't be on camera, which was a shame because she had rather a pretty face. To go with her showy blonde hair and embarrassingly large brown eyes, she had a fine, heart-shaped face and a turned-up button nose, which she thought looked like a mushroom left in the bottom of the fridge for too long. (It didn't; it was a perfectly nice nose but she'd taken against it in the way some people just don't like mice or sprouts or Manchester United. Or, indeed, clowns.)

Dad liked to take pictures of Nat's pretty face but that had been too embarrassing to allow for ages now. Recently all his photos of her looked like she was a criminal coming out of court, with either her hand over the camera lens or her duffel coat over her head.

She tried to get comfortable on her branch but a twig poked her in the eye.

Any lip readers watching the local news that night would see a furious eleven-year-old girl saying words that eleven-year-old girls shouldn't even KNOW, let alone use. Actually, Nat didn't know what they meant, but she'd heard Mum use them on Dad in the past and they seemed to help her.

They *were* quite bad though. The lady who writes the telly subtitles for the hard of hearing fainted twice. Nat closed her eyes, clung on to her branch and tried to remember how they'd got here.

HALF AN HOUR EARLIER...

Nat had been keeping her head down in case anyone saw her in the Atomic Dustbin, waiting for her chance to hop out and escape. At last the van came to a halt, engine chugging asthmatically. Nat peeked out of the window, ready to make a run for it. She was surprised to see the houses and shops and traffic lights had vanished, replaced by hedges and trees and stone walls and fields. Dad's back double had taken them on to a winding country lane. Nat didn't even know there was a country lane around here, wound or unwound.

LANES? FIELDS? Nat started to panic. Their new house was not near any *fields*. Had she been asleep under the table? Had Dad pootled obliviously on to a ferry, or driven through the Channel tunnel? Were they now ABROAD? She half expected to see a pyramid through the back window.

It was like that trip they had in the summer when Dad had tried to convince them that Dorset Council Waste Management and Sewage Centre was actually Stonehenge.

"Dad, we're really, really late," she yelled.

"You're right, I am a bit."

That worried Nat. Why would Dad say HE was late? Dad was never late because he didn't have a job to be late *for*.

On the rare occasions anyone asked her what her dad did for a living, Nat just fibbed. If the person asking had never met Dad, she might say he was a deep-sea diver, a detective, a professional footballer, a record producer, a fighter pilot or a polar explorer. If they HAD met Dad, she had to think of a lie they would believe.

She either said he built sheds or sold flowers out of a bucket.

And even that was pushing it on the credibility front. It was just really hard to believe that anyone would pay Dad money to do *anything*. For a start, he was always incredibly scruffy. It didn't matter what he wore. He could wear the most expensive suit and it would look like a hobo had found an expensive suit in some bins and was trying it on for size. Dad was just born scruffy. Mum said he even looked scruffy in the bath.

And he was too absent-minded to be trusted with a real job. You couldn't send him to the shops for a comic and a bar of Fruit and Nut, because he'd come back with a bag of apples, a trampoline and a rotary hedge-trimmer. Which

Mum would then chuck in the van out of the way.

Actually, Dad did have a job, but it was far too embarrassing to mention.

Dad wrote the jokes in Christmas crackers.

"Your dad's been responsible for ruining more Christmases than toy makers who don't include batteries," Mum told Nat one day. Which Nat thought was a bit harsh until she read some of Dad's jokes.

Why did the escapologist quit? He didn't want to be tied down.

What do you call a man with rabbits up his bottom? Warren.

Why did the baker's hands smell? Because he kneaded a poo.

The only crackers Nat ever liked were the ones that were made in China that time. The jokes came back lost in translation.

My dog has honour to have no nose? What is it that he will be smelling? Awfulness, if you please.

What's brown with stickiness? Twigs.

Sailing the seas depends on the helmsman,

waging revolution depends on Chairman Mao thought. Merry Christmas, Capitalist dogs.

Dad nearly got the sack after that; not because it was his fault but because he told the cracker bosses that he *saw the funny side*. Mum told him rather sternly it might be useful if he didn't put all his (and she said this next word very pointedly) *talents* in one basket and to get himself another job on the side.

But even when she said it, Mum didn't have much hope. What absolutely made it impossible for Dad to get a real job like everybody else's dad was that he thought EVERYTHING WAS FUNNY. Including himself. But life, as Nathalia knew, wasn't funny, not one little bit. Especially with a dad who thinks it is.

Apparently it's amusing for Nan to drop her false teeth into the Yorkshire pudding batter mix and not 'fess up until you've finished dinner.

It's comical to get pushed so hard on the swing that you fly off and land face first in the paddling pool.

It's completely hysterical to get locked out of your holiday chalet wearing only a beach towel, which then gets whipped away by the rotten Dog.

So presumably it's side-splittingly, pant-wettingly HILARIOUS to be chased up a tree by a savage goose, while your father is dressed as a clown, while the world watches you.

But that was later.

For now, Nat was still looking out of the window at the fields where Dad had just pulled over, presumably to get a map out. They were lost, and she was mega late. And even if she jumped out she wouldn't know which way to go. She looked around for landmarks, like they were told to in geography lessons. Bridge, church, woods, pylon, clown in the front seat.

CLOWN IN THE FRONT SEAT????

Nat screamed.

"It's only me, daft girl," Dad chuckled, seeing the funny side of her near heart attack. "I'm writing an article about what it's like to be a children's entertainer. I'm doing research. Meet Mister Chuckles. I'm due at the petting zoo in half an hour, and thought it best to change now, while we've stopped. Why are you trying to get out of the van?"

If he thinks Mister Chuckles is dropping me off within a mile of the school gates, he's barmy, Nathalia thought, rattling the door handle. Time to bale out. Of course, the handle was stuck. Nothing of Dad's ever worked properly.

"I don't want to alarm you…" said Dad in a voice that meant BE HUGELY ALARMED. WHAT I'M ABOUT TO SAY IS PHENOMENALLY ALARMING. GET READY TO PANIC.

"…but Ned is ever so slightly on fire."

Nathalia screamed and finally forced open the slidy door. She shot out like a cork from a bottle of fizz, followed by a cruet set, a tent and the Dog. She looked around. Through the smoke – smoke? *Smoke!!* – she saw there were no other vehicles coming down the road to rescue them. By now Dad was outside. He lifted up the red-hot and at the goose and the smoking van and at his clown gear, and threw his head back and roared with laughter.

Nat aimed a conker at his nose.

CHAPTER THREE

••••

EVENTUALLY, ONCE THE GOOSE HAD GOT BORED AND the van had stopped smoking, Nathalia and Dad and the shamed Dog and Ned the Atomic Dustbin and a young German hitch-hiker called Jurgen who had just been in the wrong place at the wrong time, approached the school gates.

The unfortunate Jurgen, trapped between a kitchen unit and a tin bath, was regretting the lift. "*Danke,*" he said. "I get out now, please." He pushed the Dog off his numb legs and tried to stand. He hit his head on something sharp and sat down again, dizzy. Nathalia thought she saw his lip tremble.

"I vill pay you to let me go."

"He's just got a mild concussion from when I stopped to pick him up and slightly ran him over," said Dad cheerfully. "I'll pop him up to Accident and Emergency after I drop you off."

Nathalia stared at the pale, miserable tourist, who was looking for something to be sick in. *Welcome to my world, Jurgen*, she thought. *Welcome to my world.*

"People say I'm lucky to be an only child," she said, "because I get ALL Dad's attention. Then they meet him."

Jurgen nodded, in between dry heaves. "Zere is such a zing as – *hueer* – too much attention."

Then Nat heard the telltale squeal of the brakes. Dad had started to turn into the school drive…

"Dad, NO! What are you doing? Don't go in, just drop me off. Preferably two streets away. DAD…"

"Don't be silly, love, you've made us late enough as it is."

"*I've* made us late? I'VE MADE US LATE??"

"Well it was you who insisted we waited for the breakdown van," replied Dad. "I told you once the engine had cooled Ned would be fine."

"Ned is NOT fine. The breakdown man said it was the worst vehicle he'd seen in his ENTIRE LIFE. And he came from Something-Stan, where they make cars from empty bean tins and roof tiles."

Dad laughed. "You do make me laugh," he said unnecessarily. "Here we are. I'll just find a space to park. It's no bother."

There was a crunching noise.

"Don't worry, the wing mirrors on those new cars are designed to snap off like that."

Dad finally found a space. It had a sign by it that read:

RESERVED FOR D HUNNY, DEPUTY HEAD. (BA, MA, PGCE, DIP ED. *MISS)*

"You can't park here, Dad."

"It's only for a few minutes, while I take you inside."

"WHAT? You're not coming in with me."

"I'll need to explain why you're so late. It's very nearly lunch time."

But Nathalia was already standing outside on the tarmac. She shut the door on Jurgen, who pressed his white face against the glass in despair.

"Just write me a note. Tomorrow. Loveyoumissyoubye..." and off she ran into the school.

In the staff room, two pinch-faced teachers watched Nathalia from an open window as they sipped whatever liquid it was that the coffee machine had given them.

Late, thought Miss Austen. *I don't like late pupils. I'll keep an eye on her.*

She's running, thought Miss Eyre. *Seems a bit keen to me. I don't like pupils thinking they're teacher's pet. I'll keep an eye on her.*

But then the caretaker Mr MacAnuff walked

past the window with just a vest on and they both decided to keep an eye on him instead.

Miss Austen sniffed her drink. "This coffee substitute smells even worse than usual," she said, wrinkling her nose and causing her face powder to shower down on to her frilly white blouse. "It smells like smoke and engine oil."

"I thought it was an improvement," said Miss Eyre, not taking her eyes off Mr MacAnuff. He seemed to be bent double and coughing, as if, for example, he'd suddenly breathed in a load of smoke and engine oil.

Nathalia reached the main school doors. They towered above her. She realised they were much bigger than the ones at her last school. She felt very small. In her old school she had known where everything was and how everything worked. Now she was starting again.

Maybe it would be different this time! She had always quite liked the IDEA of school. She thought it probably *could* be OK, if it wasn't for

Dad embarrassing her all the time.

Like the Dads' 100-metres race at her last school's Sports Day that had ended up with him in casualty, or the school barbecue that had ended up with him in the burns unit, or the school fete that had ended up with him in court. Disaster just seemed to follow Dad around.

Nat was a bright girl – like her mum – so school shouldn't have been a problem for her. Nat wasn't like Dad. She didn't like *jokes*. She liked *facts*. Though admittedly this was mostly so she could know more than him, to prove he was wrong about everything. Once at primary school this had nearly backfired on her because she learned so many facts that her school wanted to move her up a year. That would have been a definite social disaster, with or without the most embarrassing dad in the world. So when the exams came round, she wrote answers like:

Name the six wives of Henry the Eighth – Beyonce, Cleopatra, Parmesan, Fabreeze, Bilbo and my Nan.

What are the two books of the bible? – The old testicle and the new testicle.

What comes out of a volcano? – Hot saliva.

And so on. She would never admit it to herself, but she rather enjoyed doing it. When the results came out she didn't move up a year, though she still came third in her class, just below the boy who could shove eight crayons up his nose.

I should go to a better school, she had thought.

Well, now she WAS at a better school. *Better and much, much bigger*, she thought, looking up at the huge doors in front of her. *OK, Nat*, she told herself sternly, *yes, you're the new girl and yes, you've got no friends and yes, you're three hours late and yes, you've kidnapped a German in the car park and yes, everyone's going to stare at you, but it's a new start and if you can just keep Dad out of the way for the next five years you might be in with a chance of making a go of it…*

She took a deep breath and pushed at the doors. Nothing. They were shut tight. There was a keypad and little button to press and so she buzzed for attention. The intercom crackled.

"Sorry I'm late but can I come in, please?"

"This is an automatic entry system," said the robotic voice from the speaker by the door. "Welcome to school. Please select from the following options. If you are a pupil, say 'I'm a pupil.'"

Bit weird, but that was the way the day was going, so whatever.

"I'm a pupil."

"If you're a new pupil say 'I'm a new pupil.'"

"I'm a new pupil."

"If you're a girl say 'I'm a smelly girl.'"

"I'm a girl."

"You missed something out."

"Really?"

"Come on, I haven't got all day."

"Are you sniggering?" Could robots snigger?

"Just say it, say it…"

"All right, I'm a smelly girl."

"If you have long blonde hair, stand on one leg and say—"

Just then another voice, female and stern, cut in. "Come away from that intercom, you silly child."

"Come away from that intercom, you silly child," repeated Nathalia, balancing on one leg, now thoroughly confused.

There was a very nasty pause. The door buzzed open and the stern female voice said:

"Darius Bagley, you little monster, see me in my office after school. You, new girl, come in, and come into my office, now. First on the left."

And so a few minutes later, Nathalia was standing in front of Miss Hunny's desk getting her first proper telling-off of her school career. Nat didn't pay much attention, although she looked like she was taking it in and was truly sorry for her many terrible crimes. She'd learned that trick from Dad. She was *actually* thinking it must be nearly time for lunch but the smell from the kitchens wasn't all that great. A sign on the way into the school said, "Today's special is lasagne." It smelled like it was being cooked in motor oil.

Burble, burble, went the Deputy Head. Nat, drifting off, wondered if she was frowning. She was always frowning these days and Dad said she would end up with a big frowny crease in her head, like an alien or a folded blanket. That worried her and made her frown more. Bother. She lifted her eyebrows. Then she realised she probably now looked very surprised and wasn't sure if that was appropriate because she hadn't been listening. She moved her face about a bit and hoped for the best.

"Do you need to go to the toilet?" asked Miss Hunny.

"Several times a day, miss," Nathalia said, still distracted.

"Are you trying to be funny?"

Nat looked so shocked that Miss Hunny wondered what she'd said. She couldn't have known that Nat NEVER tried to be funny. 'Trying to be funny' was what Dad did ALL THE TIME, and it was embarrassing. Even Dad's favourite TV programmes were all trying to be funny.

Nat liked the news. All the news tried to be was the news. And it *was* the news, every time. Every so often Dad would think he could do better and he'd write a funny TV script and send it off. Then he'd wait until he got the usual letter telling him to get lost and he'd stomp grumpily around the house for a week and only watch animal documentaries. And when he started watching his funny programmes again he'd do a lot of tutting.

"...for the rest of your life," finished Miss Hunny. There was a pause.

"Well, what do you think?" she asked. Nathalia, caught on the hop, said the first thing that popped into her head.

"I think you're younger and prettier than your voice, miss."

"What a strange girl you are," said Miss Hunny, reddening. She might have said more but a young man in a vest burst into the room.

"If you hear the fire alarms go off, it's nothing to be worried about," said Mr MacAnuff the caretaker, reddening himself, and looking down at the floor. Nat thought he looked a bit shy. "It's just some idiot parent in the car park. His van's on fire."

Nathalia stayed at the back of the crowd of kids and teachers that had gathered around Dad's smouldering van. Someone elbowed her in the ribs. It was a scruffy little boy with a haircut that managed to be both short AND untidy. He had a jumper with an egg stain down the front and what looked like a baked bean up his nose. The creature twitched and shuffled like someone had come along with a pair of wires and hooked him up to the mains.

Darius Bagley held out a grubby hand with a stick of chewing gum in it. "Have – some – gum," he said in a suspiciously familiar robot voice.

Nat narrowed her eyes. She was going to say her dad didn't allow her to chew gum but instead she took it, feeling the thrill of rebellion at the same time as vowing revenge on the strange creature in front of her.

Some of the teachers, whose cars were being blackened by the smoke, were becoming less of a crowd and more of an angry mob, as Dad tried to calm the situation by telling everyone to "see the funny side". Soon Miss Hunny's voice could be heard rising above the general racket, as she pushed her way to the front.

"I leave my car at home for ONE DAY…" she heard the deputy head mutter. "What monstrous buffoon has parked that heap of junk there?"

That would be my dad, thought Nathalia. *My dad the monstrous buffoon. At least he's in for it now, and not me*, she added to herself. Things were looking up.

And then things started to look much, much down.

"Ivor?" said Miss Hunny, seeing Dad through the smoke. She broke into a smile.

"Dolores?" said Dad, grinning. "I've not seen you in YEARS!"

"I can't believe you've still got that horrible old van!"

And they BOTH STARTED LAUGHING.

Ha ha flipping ha, thought Nat.

Laughter was now ringing out across the playground. Kids, teachers, even the German backpacker was seeing the funny side. Nat realised that she had only been at her new school for five minutes and already the whole place was laughing and she was the only one who didn't get the joke. Which must mean that, once again, the joke was massively on her.

Then she realised her dad had been right about not chewing gum because she started to choke on it.

CHAPTER FOUR

· · · ·

THE SAINT JOHN AMBULANCE-APPROVED METHOD of rescuing someone who is choking on a bit of chewing gum does NOT include tipping them upside down and vigorously shaking it out.

Which is what Darius Bagley did to Nathalia as she gasped and turned a nasty shade of purple. Or rather, it's what he *tried* to do. But Darius was five centimetres shorter than Nat, so he only succeeded in knocking her flat and banging her head on the tarmac. This made her so furious she let loose a great yell and expelled the bit of gum, smack in his left eye. Darius went down like a stone and Nat was on him in a flash, all flailing hair and tiny fists of fury. She managed to get a few swift kicks in before she was dragged away by Miss Eyre, who had come to see what all the fuss was about.

Miss Eyre waited until Nat had delivered a particularly solid whack before dragging her away. She'd quite liked to have got a few toe-pokes in on Darius herself but that'd been banned by schools for ages so watching Nat do it was the next best thing.

"I can see you're going to be trouble," she said to Nat. *Oh, today just gets better and better,* thought Nat.

Darius scrambled to his feet as Miss Eyre lifted Nathalia off the ground, wriggling and hissing. "Not bad for a girl," said Darius, dusting himself off and feeling his ribs carefully. "But not much thanks for saving your life."

Nathalia eyed her new nemesis suspiciously. She wondered if just maybe he was right and he'd got the kicking she secretly wanted to give someone else…

That person, of course, was still chatting happily to Miss Hunny, over by the smouldering vehicle.

"Detention, both of you," barked Miss Eyre.

"That's right," simpered Miss Austen, sidling up.

"Not fair," shouted Darius correctly.

"Yeah, it is," said Nathalia, confusing everyone.

"I think we all know Darius well enough to know it will be mostly his fault," said Miss Eyre.

"You always say that," said Darius, outraged. "You even said it on my first day."

"Your other school wrote to us," she replied sweetly. "Enclosing reports."

"And photographs," added Miss Eyre.

"And newspaper clippings," added Miss Austen.

"And don't forget," said Miss Eyre, her tone darkening, "that this school has endured your older brother... Oswald," finished Miss Eyre at last, lowering her voice to a terrified whisper, as if even saying his name might conjure him up.

"Now what's happening here?" said Miss Hunny, who had in fact appeared instead of Oswald Bagley. "Darius, off to the Head's office. Nathalia, not you." She turned to Nathalia. "Your father tells me you're easily led. Perhaps you should be a little more careful who you hang around with in future."

Nathalia glared at her dad, who winked at her, chuffed for getting her off a detention. Then she saw poor Darius Bagley being marched off to Mrs Trout's office. He suddenly looked tiny against the looming new school buildings and then he was swallowed up by the kids milling about in the playground, jostling and shouting.

With all the fuss, Nat had missed lunch, so it was with heavy heart and light stomach that she trooped into her very first lesson that afternoon. It was maths. *Of course it would be maths*, she thought to herself sourly. *Can this day get any worse?*

Well yes it can, she answered herself, a microsecond later. As she entered the classroom she could see that all the kids had put dibs on desks way back at the start of the school year. There they all sat, chatting away with their chums. Nat felt very alone – and very stared at – as she walked in. She tried to put a brave face on it, but then she caught a glimpse of her reflection in a window and realised her face was covered in grime from the Atomic Dustbin. The tittering had already begun as she looked around for a place to sit.

She knew she had one last chance to rescue the day that Dad had officially ruined. If she could sit next to a popular girl, she might just…

Oh no. There was one empty chair. It was at the back, next to the one kid nobody wanted to sit with. Darius Bagley.

He hadn't seen her yet because his attention was totally taken up with what was up his left nostril. It looked like he was trying to get his *entire* finger in.

He worked away squeakily for a minute or two, not noticing Nat, who was desperately looking for another chair to sit on. ANY chair. Get the right friend now and she'd be set for her whole school career. Must – find – the – right – friend. Faces of the children swam before her, strangers but already familiar; the pretty one, the clever one, the sporty one, the silly one, the rude one, any would do, but none of them sat next to an empty chair. Suddenly there was a horrible squelching sound and Darius triumphantly produced a crusty, glistening pen top.

There was no other seat. She sighed and took her place next to him. He put the top back on his pen and stared at her. She stared back.

Darius thought for a minute. When Darius Bagley thought, which was not often, he usually chewed his pen top.

He chewed his bogey-ed pen top. And pulled a face.

Nathalia started to giggle.

This surprised her because Dad never made her laugh and he was officially hilarious, according to Dad.

Darius spat out the pen top at the back of Margaret Mortimer's head, where it stuck.

Nathalia laughed so hard she almost fell off her chair.

But later on in maths Darius Bagley did something very strange. It wasn't his handstands – they were just funny. It wasn't the size of the snot bubbles he could create and pop at the drop of a hat – they were just gross. Nathalia didn't even find Darius's farmyard-animal impressions strange. She very quickly realised he was the kind of kid who could be relied upon to snort and cluck and moo at the right moment. For example, whenever the teacher wasn't looking.

No; what was really, properly strange about Darius was this.

It was towards the end of the lesson and Mr Frantz, the harassed elderly maths teacher, had just dragged the quacking, handstanding, bogey-popping Darius from out of the book cupboard for the second time.

"You are a disgrace to this school, to your parents and to the noble and ancient art of mathematics," said Mr Frantz, who was German and tended to wave his arms around a lot. Right now he was keeping them busy by waving them around even more than usual, because if left to their own devices his hands would have found themselves round Darius's throat, enjoying a gentle throttle. Mr Frantz snatched up Darius's work from his desk, wiped various unidentified unpleasantnesses off it, and read.

"You have not done the sitting still more than five minutes. You have done NO work. When I look at this all I see is…"

There was a pause. The class waited, knowing what was coming next.

"All I see is..."

OK, *now you're milking it*, thought Nathalia. *Tell him off and get it over with.*

"Every single sum is… is correct."

He read everything again. "Correct?" Mr Frantz looked up and glared at Nathalia, who was still stuck on question six.

"Miss Hunny tells me you are a very clever girl."

Nathalia's heart sank as all the other children, who had lost interest in Darius now he wasn't going to be roasted alive, turned and stared at her instead. *Thanks AGAIN, Dad*, she thought. *Another winner.*

"You must not help this chimp of a boy. It will do him no good and the only job he will be getting is in the circus or presenting television programmes."

Darius wasn't listening though. He was trying to unscrew the desk lid with a tiny knife. Mr Frantz snatched the knife off him.

"Detention this break," he said to Darius.

"Already got one."

"Well, sit twice as still."

Mr Frantz marched back to his own desk where he pretended to read a maths textbook. He was actually working out if he could afford to retire yet. The answer didn't please him. Nathalia looked at Darius's paper in awe.

"How...?" she began. He had literally spent two non-chimp minutes all lesson.

"Dunno," he said, rolling something green into a ball. Nathalia told herself it could be Plasticine. "It's just obvious."

The last lesson of the day was English, and the teacher was the dreaded Miss Hunny. Nat used to quite like English. It was the one lesson where staring out of the window blankly, enjoying a nice daydream, was encouraged. And it was easy too. She once wrote a story about Stingy Eric, a wasp the size of a bus. You didn't need to know how clouds were formed to know that clouds full of boiling radioactive acid would melt Stingy Eric into a big yellow and black waspy blob.

But now English was ruined, thanks to stupid Dad and Miss flipping Hunny. Her dad – and her teacher – WERE FRIENDS. And all the class knew it. It was only one step away from being *related* to a teacher, which was social death. And here she was, all sickly sweet at the front of the class, trilling over some poetry about daffodils. She imagined Stingy Eric zooming in, bum end first, right for Miss—

Nat became dimly aware that Miss Hunny was talking to her. Yet again she had no idea what to say. She went with:

"Yes."

'Yes' was usually safe because everyone likes to be agreed with.

"Well go on then," said Miss Hunny pleasantly, then after a quiet moment or two, "I have it on very good authority that Nathalia is an excellent reader. Borderline genius, I've been told."

More glares from classmates that were in danger of becoming classfoes. *Thanks again, Dad*, thought Nat, mentally sending stingy Eric on another mission.

"You know where we are, don't you?"

She didn't. Darius casually jabbed a dirty finger on the poetry book they were sharing. She wondered if she trusted him. She wasn't a natural truster. It came from listening to her nan, known to all the family as Bad News Nan. She'd learned not to trust:

Strangers, postmen, Sky News, the French, women in make-up, the water abroad, banks, the government, men with beards, men in hats, men with glasses, men in general. Pot noodles, weather girls, Prince Charles, helicopters, the internet, Greeks Bearing Gifts, footballers, vegetarians, soap stars, Radio One, gangsta rappers and boys who work on the fairground rides.

It was a tricky decision; Nan had never met Darius Bagley but she'd probably have put him on the DO NOT TRUST list right next to Snoop Doggy Dogg.

However, Nathalia didn't seem to have a lot of choice, so she started reading from the mark Darius's sticky finger had left behind.

It wasn't just the wrong *line*, it was the wrong *poem*. She was wondering what a burning tiger was doing in all the daffodils, but then again Stingy Eric once went to Tesco. Miss Hunny frowned, the class laughed and Nat knew she'd been tricked. She felt a sense of relief along with shame. There had been enough new things for her to get to grips with that day; maybe trusting Darius Bagley would have been one too many. She stamped on his foot and poked him in the eye.

"I'm very disappointed in you," said Miss Hunny gently. She'd kept Nathalia back for 'a quiet word' after class at the end of the day. Nathalia was surprised it actually *was* quiet. The last time Mum told Dad she wanted a 'quiet word', people three doors down complained about the noise.

An acrid petrol smell alerted Nat that the Atomic Dustbin was in the general area. Nat fidgeted, not listening, eager to escape. She should have been paying more attention, but all she heard were Miss Hunny's final words: "... but your father says you're very well behaved at home. I suppose I'll see for myself on Friday."

Nathalia was halfway down the corridor before she realised with horror what Miss Hunny must have meant. Thanks to Dad, HER TEACHER WAS COMING TO HER HOUSE.

CHAPTER FIVE

• • • •

NAT WANTED TO TALK TO HER MUM ABOUT MISS HUNNY coming for tea. Mum would understand it was IMPOSSIBLE to have her teacher round. She just needed to get Mum on her own. She knew that parents always agreed with each other IN FRONT OF THE CHILDREN, so the way to get what you wanted was to ask each of them separately, and keep going from one to the other until you got the right answer. Sadly, Nat never got the chance to get Mum on her own. Mum came home early and to celebrate Nat's first day whisked them all off for a Chinese and a trip to the cinema, ON A SCHOOL NIGHT, GET IN.

Nat loved it when Mum was home because they always did fun things. Mum had a knack of getting whatever she wanted, which was the opposite of Dad, who just got what he got given. And was happy about it. Nat saw that as more proof of how rubbish Dad was.

Also, when Mum said they were going out for a Chinese and to see the new James Bond, they were guaranteed a sweet and sour chicken/ action film combo evening. When Nathalia went out with Dad, she never knew *what* was going to happen. They might end up on a bouncy castle, they might end up in Belgium. It drove her bananas.

Nat was in bed and dropping off to sleep, Mum's perfume still lingering from her goodnight kiss, before she realised she hadn't had the chance to talk about her wretched teacher. *Oh well*, she thought, *I've got all week*. She dreamt Darius Bagley and Dolores Hunny were chasing her around the playground with a pair of killer chopsticks.

She was half-woken by Mum saying goodbye early the next morning, pale spring sunlight filtering weakly through the curtains.

"Go back to sleep," whispered Mum, kissing her hair.

"Can you write me a note to get me off hockey," said Nat, remembering she had games today. At least that's what she thought she said, but her voice was thick with sleep.

"Yes, I love you too," said Mum. "See you on Saturday."

Saturday. *Saturday????* Suddenly Nat was wide awake. "What?"

"Sorry, forgot to say, I'm staying up this week. I know it's your first week at school but it's my first week at my new job too and I have to make a good first impression. You know what that's like."

Yes I do, thought Nat. *But it's too late for me.*

Go, Mum, save yourself.

Mum looked sad and Nat didn't want to worry her so she didn't say anything about her own troubles. Mum kissed her again. "There's a work thing – it's too boring to talk about. But we'll do something nice on the weekend, I promise."

I doubt it, thought Nat, *if Dad brings my teacher here, I'll be on the run for killing him to death.*

They were only ten minutes late that morning as the Atomic Dustbin only broke down once. Fortunately it was at a busy set of traffic lights, so there were plenty of people only too willing to push it down the road to get it started again.

"That was handy, attracting that large crowd," said Dad, as they wheezed along. "Nat? Nat? Where are you?"

Nat came out from under the table once the shouting and swearing had faded away. Now she could only hear the annoying morning DJs. There were three of them – Kerri, Bonehead and Cabbage. They were busy entertaining themselves by making prank phone calls. They were talking to a young woman who worked in an 'Everything's a Pound' shop.

"How much are your disposable barbecues?" asked Bonehead.

"A pound." Kerri and Cabbage sniggered on air.

"So If I buy TWO disposable barbecues, but then get to the till and decide to put one back, how much will that be?" said Kerri.

"A pound. Everything's a pound."

Cabbage and Bonehead chortled. Now it was Cabbage's turn.

"How about three disposable barbecues? In case I want to buy two as presents? I'm not sure I have enough money. How much will three disposable barbecues cost?"

"Three pounds," said the shop girl heavily.

"You've been PRANKED!" shouted the DJs, laughing hysterically.

"Oh, right," said the woman from the

'Everything's a Pound' shop. "Does that mean you don't want any disposable barbecues? Only there's a big queue now."

Dad burst out laughing. "Some people," he said. "You couldn't make it up."

Nat hated Kerri, Bonehead and Cabbage because they were idiots and because they didn't play enough music, but Dad put them on because they'd all gone to college together. Nat thought Dad was a tiny bit jealous, and probably always thought he could have been a DJ too.

"I'll ring THEM up one day," he said, chuckling. "I'll turn the tables on them. You won't believe it but we got up to some really embarrassing things when we were at college."

"I believe it, Dad," said Nat, panicking. "Please don't ring them."

She decided to QUICKLY change the subject. She asked Dad if he could write her a note getting her off hockey. She could get a note for anything off the big softie. Especially after she spent five minutes buttering him up and telling him what a great DJ he was.

Now, that WAS a fib. Nat had seen Dad's DJ'ing. Nan once won first prize at the bingo and took them all to a holiday camp in Wales. On day two, the man who did the disco ran off with the runner-up of the Miss Prestatyn competition and Dad offered to take over for free. He spent a happy week dancing with glow-sticks and shouting about the funky train. People started recognising him around the pool and pointing. Nat hid in her chalet and Mum booked herself into a B&B down the road. Nat had made him promise NEVER to DJ again. So far so good, but she didn't trust him one bit...

Saying she wasn't 'feeling well enough to do hockey' WASN'T a fib. She wasn't sure HOW well she'd have to feel to want to do hockey, but it was definitely weller than this. Plus, if it WAS a crime to fib, this fib was a crime without a victim. She didn't have to play hockey; the school didn't have to put up with the world's worst hockey player. Everyone's a winner.

As they pulled into the school car park, Nat grabbed the note off Dad and ran up the drive just ahead of Darius Bagley, who was being dropped off on A MOTORBIKE. Nathalia stopped, stunned. Part of her thought it was incredibly stupid and dangerous and probably not allowed, but another, jealous part of her thought it was just amazingly cool. It was less cool when she saw Darius picking flies out of his teeth.

The huge thing in black leathers straddling the noisy black bike might have been a human being but Nat doubted it. For a start, it was another Bagley. All she could see under the helmet were thick black sunglasses and thick black hair. The creature roared off, making Dad in the Atomic Dustbin swerve violently to avoid a crash.

"Hello, Bumhole," said Darius, blowing a traumatised bug from his left nostril, "that's my brother, Oswald."

Nat froze. Fortunately, no one had heard Darius say her infamous name. She had to act fast. She grabbed him by his scruffy blazer.

"Don't EVER call me Bumhole," she said. "No one knows." Amazingly, when Miss Hunny had read out her name the day before, she'd said it properly – Bew-mole-ay. No one had seen her last name written down yet either, so only Darius had worked out what it actually looked like.

"What's it worth?" he said.

"Not being pinched every day until Year Thirteen," she replied dangerously.

"Might be worth it," he said, laughing as she chased him into school.

Nat thought she'd better sit next to Darius in class, to make sure he didn't spill the beans about her name, at least not until she'd made some friends. This wasn't difficult, as no one else wanted to sit with him.

The class had been set maths homework over the Easter break. Mr Frantz handed it back to them that morning. Nat noticed Darius had got minus five per cent.

"You got nought per cent for not doing it, and minus five per cent for spelling your name wrong," explained Mister Frantz. He was in a bad mood because he knew he had Darius first thing and he didn't have a dad to write him a sick note.

"You can do all these in two minutes," said Nat, puzzled and a little irritated. Darius rolled the final spitty bug into a little ball and flicked it at Mr Frantz's back.

"Course I can. So I don't have to," he said logically.

Nat worked away at her desk for a while, trying to make x equal something less than six million when she knew there wasn't a right-angled triangle that big anywhere in the known universe, when Darius poked her in the ribs.

"I am less than a metre away from you, moron," she snapped, "you can get my attention without causing me bodily harm."

"Write me a note to get off games?" he asked. "You've got nice writing."

"Are you ill?" she replied, doing her best Mum impression.

"No, I just don't wanna do games."

"The rest of us have to do it," said Nathalia primly, not mentioning her own note.

"I WILL tell you why x is fifteen," he said. "And I WON'T tell everyone your last name."

"Deal. How ill do you want to be?"

They eventually settled on 'too ill for games and just this side of the intensive care unit and isn't he brave for struggling into school despite all this illness which isn't catching by the way so in case there's a school trip on the cards somewhere fun like a castle or amusement park he can definitely still go, sort of ill'.

When she'd finished, Nathalia was quite proud of her note. She wanted to sign it and asked what his mum's name was. Darius frowned and made a funny sort of shrug and kicked one of his shoes off under his desk. He had holes in his sock.

"Just put Mister Bagley," he said. For a

second he looked tiny and alone and Nat had a strange urge to put her arm round him. Then she saw what he was doing with his hands and swiftly decided against it.

CHAPTER SIX

• • • •

MISS HUNNY TOOK THEM FOR HOCKEY – ANOTHER REASON Nathalia was trying to avoid it. Now, there are two sorts of teachers who do games. The first are the lumpy ones in shabby tracksuits who can actually run and throw and kick and jump and catch and all that. At one time they wanted to be in the Olympics but liked cigarettes, beer, cake, pork scratchings and Sunday lie-ins a bit too much. These days they still like sports, but they hate kids.

The other sort are the proper teachers who

teach a real subject who like kids and like playing games with them. These teachers are a mixed blessing. They are much nicer, but they are rubbish at sport and are just as likely to knock your nose off with a badly swung hockey stick as not. Miss Hunny was one of those.

As everyone piled into the changing rooms, Nathalia handed Miss Hunny the note from her dad. She wondered if anyone was in the library. Some of the well-thumbed books reserved for the Year Tens with black covers and vampires looked pretty interesting.

"Well hurry up then," said Miss Hunny brightly, waving the note. "I'm looking forward to seeing what you can do."

Betrayed, thought Nat, miserably grabbing Dad's note back. She read:

Dear Dolores,

My daughter is a very talented little girl. Her one fault is being too modest. I know she's great at sports because she's got the high scores on the Wii Olympics.

And when she plays catch with her little cousin Marcus she usually wins. even though he's quite big for a five-year-old. I've got a wonderful video of her on a beach last year. She'd just dropped an ice cream down her pants and it shows how high she can jump when she puts her mind to it.

At her old school she'd even pretend to be ill just to let others take all the glory but it's time she got the attention she deserves.

Looking forward to seeing you on Friday. I'll cook: it will be like old times. Except this time hopefully you won't get food poisoning.

Love Ivor (Bumolé)

That's the last time I ask my stupid dad for a note, she fumed, pulling her kit on. *I don't care. I could have two broken arms and the bubonic plague and I still wouldn't make that mistake again.*

She ran on to the playing field with the other girls and wondered who would be worse than her. Her plan was to stand next to that girl all lesson. But to her dismay, most of the girls looked super fit and keen. Some were already warming up, WITHOUT BEING TOLD. One girl was even doing press-ups. Nat sighed. *Where's the pale crying girl with glasses?* she wondered. *There must be at least one.*

It started drizzling.

They were now huddled together in the middle of the pitch and Nat was surprised to see that they were sharing the lesson with the boys. She looked, but couldn't see Darius, which meant her note must have worked. Oh hang on, no, here he came, trudging sulkily on to the field in old, baggy shorts and a stained top. He hissed at her as he walked past.

"So now I've got games AND a double detention. Thanks a lot."

"Yeah, well, thanks to my dad, my note was worse, dog-breath."

They weren't taking any notice of Miss Hunny, burbling away in the background. "We're looking at basic ball control and tackling," they might have heard, if they'd been listening.

"I had a more rubbish note than you did," argued Darius.

"It was me who had the worst one," Nathalia snapped back. This boy was really ungrateful.

"So can I have two volunteers?" wittered Miss Hunny.

"Me," insisted Darius loudly.

"No, me," said Nat, even louder.

"OK, Darius and Nathalia, thank you. Come here then."

"This is your fault as well," said Darius as they collected their hockey sticks. "I'm gonna shout out your name."

Nathalia wrapped her hands tight round her stick. "You are not," she said, "but you are gonna shout." She cracked him on the ankle.

"Bum – owww!" shouted Darius.

"Rude boy, another detention," shouted Miss Hunny. Darius yelped and started hopping about. "Darius, calm down. What IS the matter with you? Don't answer that – enough people have tried to work it out and failed. Right, you two, face each other."

"I don't want to look at his face," said Nat.

"I don't need to look at hers, I know what she looks like – horrible."

"Darius, you have the ball. Now, on my whistle, let's start."

There are some scenes that are so violent and disturbing, that to write them down would mean we'd need a warning sticker on the front of this book saying something like:

PARENTS BEWARE – IF YOUR CHILDREN READ THIS THEY WILL BE DAMAGED FOR LIFE. STOP! DANGER, DANGER. *DO NOT OPEN WITHOUT PROTECTIVE CLOTHING.* PLEASE DISPOSE OF THIS BOOK CAREFULLY. IF RASH DEVELOPS, SEE YOUR DOCTOR. READ LESS, WATCH TV MORE. THE VALUE OF YOUR INVESTMENTS MAY GO DOWN AS WELL AS UP. SIT UP STRAIGHT AND EAT YOUR PEAS.

So let's just listen to Miss Hunny, and work out what's happening from that.

"Darius, you try to dribble the ball past Nathalia, who has to try to stop you.

"No, I didn't say whack the ball straight at her. Nathalia, you are not allowed to pick up the ball unless you're the goalkeeper. Oh right, you're giving it back to— Not so hard! Now you've hit him in the eye. Darius, you cannot wave your stick about like a caveman. Now, you two, no swordfighting.

"No, really, you have to stop – watch that stick, you'll hit Maddie. Oh, Maddie! That sort of language might be acceptable on a football pitch but not here.

"Maddie, put Darius down.

Jamie, you needn't get involved, or you, Rajesh. Nathalia, are you biting Darius's ear? Right, everyone put down your sticks. Right now. Stop fighting. Who hit me on the— Argh! Why are you all joining in? *Stop joining in*. Put those sticks down.

Help, help. Mr MacAnuff!"

The caretaker, who always just 'happened' to be nearby whenever Miss Hunny was on the playing fields, rushed over to help. His white vest clung to him in the rain. *It's a bit tight – maybe it got shrunk in the wash,* thought Nathalia, as she was hauled out of the fight.

"You two, go and sit outside my office till the end of school," said Miss Hunny. "I'll deal with you then."

"What would your father say?" said Miss Hunny to Nat, surprisingly sternly. Nat was standing in front of Miss Hunny's desk. Her left eye felt swollen but she didn't care because Darius, standing next to her, looked worse. "You may pull the wool over his eyes but I'm beginning to see there's a very troublesome streak in you. I mean, I hardly recognise you from this photo your father texted me today."

She showed Nat her phone. With creeping horror Nat guessed what the picture would be, even before she looked. It was Dad's all-time favourite. It was her eighth birthday and she was dressed as a fairy princess. Nat wanted the ground to open up under her. Darius was trying to stop himself laughing, which made him laugh more. Stuff came out of his notorious nose and he wiped it with the back of his hand. Miss Hunny shuddered and hurried things along so she didn't have to be around him any longer.

"And take a look at yourself now," she said, holding up a mirror.

Nat looked. Her face was dirty and bruised, her left eye purple. Her hair was matted and sticking up in clumps. When she was a very little girl she had a favourite doll. She loved it so much she wouldn't let the doll out of her sight, not even to be washed. After several years it was so disgusting that Dad nicknamed it Typhoid Mary. Nat didn't know what that meant so didn't know why adults would laugh whenever she told them what it was called.

Today she didn't look like Dad's fairy princess. She looked like Typhoid Mary.

"I've decided I cannot overlook this terrible incident – Darius, stop playing with that – so I'll be calling your parents tonight."

"Good luck trying," muttered Darius. Nat looked at him. His lips were pursed tight in defiance and his face was unreadable. She thought about his horrible brother and his holey socks. And he DID help her find x…

She moved a little closer to him.

"And Nathalia, I'm seeing your poor father on Friday so we'll have plenty of time to discuss the best way of dealing with you." *Dealing?* thought Nat, pulling a face. She let out a sigh.

She felt Darius move a little closer to her.

Neither said anything as they left the classroom together and made their way towards the school gates.

In the distance Nat could see the hulking figure of Oswald Bagley approaching on his huge black motorbike.

"See you, Buttface," said Darius, walking off.

Nat smiled to herself as she heard Dad's dustbin chugging round the corner.

Buttface? she thought. *Yeah, I can live with that.*

CHAPTER SEVEN

....

On the way home, Dad made an unexpected right turn at the mini roundabout by the park. Nathalia hoped he was just getting lost again. Because if he wasn't getting lost, he was doing something far, far worse. He was taking them to the supermarket. And she was still wearing her school uniform. She squirmed at the thought and scratched the stupid Dog behind his ear. He looked at her sadly, as if to agree that even his tiny doggy brain knew you can't be seen in school uniform *outside school*. *It's bad enough*

wearing the scratchy, lumpy thing IN school, thought Nat.

The brakes squeaked and Nat risked a peek out of the window. Oh no. Or rather, oh yes, here they were, at the ticket barrier of the supermarket car park. As usual, Dad had pulled up way too far from the ticket machine. Nat watched as he stretched out his arm to get the

ticket. He couldn't reach. He stuck his head out of the window. Still couldn't reach. And now he couldn't reverse and try again because there was a small queue of cars behind him. Nat sank lower on the seat and hid behind the Dog as the first car horns started blaring. Dad was now half out of the window, his legs hovering inside. *One little push*, thought Nat, *one little—*

"Got it!" shouted Dad. Nathalia stopped moving towards the dangling legs.

"No, dropped it," shouted Dad. Nathalia started moving again.

"It's gone under the van," said Dad, coming inside, face now purple from his efforts. "Just pop out and get it, would you, love. It'll be easier for you. Just mind the exhaust – there's a small chance it might be red hot."

"Can't you do it, Dad?" she shouted over the car horns.

"I would, but I think it's best I keep the engine revved. How popular would we be if we broke down here?"

"About the same as we are now," muttered Nat under her breath, as she slid open the side door. Only a couple of pans clanged out behind her as she scrabbled under the van. As her fingers reached for the ticket, something warm and wet plopped on to the side of her face.

"What's the Dog doing?" she shouted in mild panic, but Dad couldn't hear. She snatched the ticket, banged her head on something hard and scrambled back into the van. A large smear of engine oil covered half her face, and her white school shirt was the colour of a February raincloud. She was no longer Typhoid Mary. She was the girl Typhoid Mary wasn't allowed to play with.

When they eventually found a parking space, Dad looked at his daughter. "You might need a wet wipe," he said, smiling. Nathalia was shocked. *I must look terrible for Dad to notice*, she thought. She had once come back from a fair with her face painted like a tiger and asked Dad what was different about her. After a few minutes he asked if she'd bought some new trainers.

She rubbed her sleeve over her face quickly. "Can I just stay in the van?" she asked. "Normally I'd say yes," said Dad, "but I need your advice."

Nat frowned. She liked being asked for her advice because she liked telling people what to do. She didn't get the chance to do that very often so this was a tempting offer. On the other hand, shopping with Dad was just about the worst experience she could imagine, outside of a trip to the dentist or being munched by a giant spider.

"You'll spend ages in there," she complained, as they got out of the van and weaved their way through the busy car park. "You always do."

"Not with your help," said Dad.

"You always take hours choosing the cheapest tins of beans, and looking at those beers with the stupid names like Fiddler's Armpit or Old Rat Hole."

Dad chuckled. "You got me," he said.

"The last time we went you asked that assistant if he had a Goblin's Knob and I had to hide in the frozen peas."

"You do make me laugh," said Dad, laughing. "You can push the trolley. We'll have fun."

"I'll do it if we can look at clothes." This was a gamble, because Dad HATED looking at clothes with her. But he nodded. "Good idea," he said, which puzzled her. *Ah well, he must really want my help with something*, she thought, heading for the clothing section.

She was so pleased with herself she hardly noticed they had started with the dresses. Dad held up a horrible pink fluffy thing.

"It's a bit small for Mum," said Nat.

"It's for you," said Dad. "No, don't run off – come back. Don't you want to look nice for Miss Hunny's visit?"

So that was it. AAAARGH! It wasn't that Nathalia didn't want to look nice. Obviously she didn't want to look nice for Miss Hunny, but in general, she liked to look nice. Trouble was, *her* idea of nice was very different to *Dad's* idea of nice. Dad wanted to see her in a long dress covered with flowers, bunnies or flowery bunnies. Nat's version of nice was a tiny pair of denim shorts and a T-shirt with a skull and WHAT ARE YOU LOOKING AT? emblazoned on it.

Ten minutes later Mrs Doldrums the elderly shop assistant was trying to stop the row that was now raging between Nat and her dad. She was as effective as a drama teacher breaking up a playground scrap.

Finally the two of them made it to the ladies changing rooms. Nat had an armful of clothes that Dad didn't like. Dad had an armful of clothes that he didn't like much either but were better than the ones Nat *really* liked. And Mrs Doldrums had two customers that she just hated.

When a changing room became free, Dad went to march in with Nat. Mrs Doldrums, shocked, tapped him on the arm.

"You can't go in there," she said. "It's ladies only."

"She's right, Dad, go away," said Nat, who had already decided to tell him none of the clothes he chose fitted her. She didn't want him to see that she hadn't even tried them on.

"She's my daughter," said Dad, refusing to budge.

"She'll be perfectly safe in there," replied Mrs Doldrums, through gritted false teeth.

"I know that," replied Dad. "I just need to

help her with the buttons."

Several unkind ladies in the changing rooms burst out laughing and Nat looked for a large hole to jump into.

"I can do my own buttons," she hissed. "I've been able to do them since I was six." There was more laughter.

"Will you come out of there?" said the shop assistant, who was also looking for a hole in the ground. Only this one was to push Dad into. And then chuck a fridge on.

"If you want to sell clothes, you need to look carefully at how you treat your customers," said Dad loudly. One or two of the ladies in the changing rooms clapped. Encouraged by this, Dad went off on one.

"I remember a time when the customer was always right," declared Dad to the whole shop. "I was reading in the financial papers that your profits were down eleven point six per cent last year, and I think I can see why."

Nat couldn't be sure, but she had a good idea

that Dad was fibbing. Dad never read the financial papers; he wasn't very good with numbers. All he read were books and music magazines and the little booklets inside CDs. When Mum brought home the paper he'd skim the sports pages and finish her crossword in about ten seconds – which really annoyed her – but numbers just confused him. Nat remembered a row at an ice-cream van because Dad didn't see why a 99 cost a pound.

Mrs Doldrums, who was one month away from retiring and moving to a bungalow by the seaside with her cats, did not care about the store's financial doom, real or imagined. She cared about getting Dad out of the ladies' changing rooms.

"If you don't step out of there, I'll call the manager," she said.

Oh no. Not The Manager. Nat hid her head in her hands. This was terrible. You see, on the whole Dad liked just about everybody. When they were out, Nat would have to listen, bored stiff, as he chatted happily to anyone who was prepared to chat back. Even if, she recalled only too well, it was a tramp on a bench who wanted to sell them a toaster. It usually took them an hour to walk down the high street. Teenagers who sign people up for charities would chuck themselves behind a lamp post when they saw Dad coming.

The only people Dad didn't like were people IN UNIFORM. He couldn't help it, he just hated being told what to do. (Unless it was by Mum, which slightly confused Nat.)

Nat felt sure that even if the manager wasn't in a uniform, they would still count as someone who was telling Dad what to do. She couldn't risk another long stand-off like the one at airport security last year when they tried to take a jar of jam off him. The customs people said it was a possible weapon; Dad said it was strawberry jam. Eventually he was taken into a little room for an hour and they missed their flight.

Nat knew what to do, even though she hated doing it, especially in public. But there was no other way. She put on her sweetest little girl voice and turned her sweetest ickle little girly face to her dad.

"Daddy, the clothes you like are lovely and I know they'll fit, they're the right size and everything, but I'm ever so thirsty and I really need a drink, please can we go to the café, please, Daddy?"

Thirty seconds later they were in the café. *Victory*, thought Nat, sucking on a box of juice. Sort of. Even if she did have a new wardrobe's worth of dodgy clothing.

"Righto," said Dad after they'd both got their breath back, "now it's your turn to help me." Nat groaned inside. But the next thing he said made her heart skip an evil beat.

"What can I cook for Miss Hunny? It's been ages since we saw each other; I'd like to give her something memorable."

Oooh, thank you, Dad, thought Nat, having an immediate, awesome, evil idea, *I'll make sure we give her something she'll never forget.*

CHAPTER EIGHT

• • • •

Now, DAD'S MEALS WERE FAMOUSLY RANK AT THE BEST OF times. Dad's meals were something starving celebrities would refuse to eat in a television competition. Nat reckoned they should only really be used as a method of persuading criminals to confess.

His efforts usually came out of packets and involved something pale in lots of crunchy batter. Vegetables were only ever peas (tinned), or peas (mushy), which Dad said were the King of Veg. To be fair, not everything came out of packets –

Dad was quite fond of a pie in a tin too.

He also had a huge soft spot for pickles. If there was something floating dangerously in a jar full of brown liquid at the back of the cupboard, Dad was on it in a flash. "Vinegar is nature's own wonder food," he'd say, eyeing up the last pickled egg in the chip shop greedily.

Dad's idea of a varied diet was a pork pie, some oven chips, a pickled herring, a spoon of Marmite and maybe a green ice lolly – as green was the colour of vitamins. That lasted until Nat wrote an essay about 'What I had for my tea last night' and Dad got a letter from a social worker.

But Friday's meal was going to be the worst ever – Nat was going to make sure of that. Dad was very nearly the worst cook in the world. With her help he could be the worst, and Miss Hunny would never dare to set foot in their house again.

"I suppose we could have Chinese takeaway," Dad said as they lingered over rank meats at the deli counter.

"No, we can't," said Nat loudly. Chinese was what they had with Mum. There was no way Miss Hunny was stuffing her soppy face with spring rolls and crispy duck pancakes in Mum's house, no way at all. She grabbed Dad's hand and tugged him away.

Nat's mind raced as she pulled Dad down the aisles, her GENIUS EVIL PLAN OF DOOM evolving in her head as she went. His most revolting meal of all time was something he called the Surf, Turf and Smurf Mash-up. The memory of this meal was so terrible she'd tried to block it out for over a year, but she'd failed. She swallowed hard as it all came back to her – rather like it had done when she ate it. She suddenly remembered the sight and smell and – gack, here comes a little bit of sick – *taste* of the stuff, and she felt clammy all over. Perfect.

"How about the Surf, Turf and Smurf Throw-up, I mean Mash-up?" she asked, trying to keep her voice calm.

"Really?" said Dad doubtfully. "Didn't you

make me promise never to make it again on pain of death?"

"No, I quite liked it, once I'd got used to it."

"I seem to remember there was some performance with you rolling about on the floor pretending you'd been poisoned."

"I wasn't being serious."

"You said you felt sorry for the bin when you chucked it away."

"Joke, Dad, come on. Let's get the ingredients. What was in it?"

Nat was genuinely interested to know what was in it. Her best guess so far was: flour, milk, butter, eggs, potatoes, glue, dog chews, iron filings, bran flakes, sardines, cheese, cough medicine, toothpaste, knicker elastic and a pinch of salt. And she wasn't too sure about the salt.

"I'm not convinced it was a recipe AS SUCH..." said Dad.

You surprise me, thought Nat.

"...it was more improvising on a theme."

What the heck was the theme? thought Nat,

with a shudder. *A theme from a horror film, perhaps.* But Dad was now wandering round the aisles with that familiar blank expression that meant he was looking for something. "There were definitely some frozen prawns and a meat pie filling in the mix somewhere," said Dad, dragging his eyes from the shelves of beer. *Sounds about right*, thought Nat, already feeling a bit queasy.

Half an hour later, their trolley was full. Nat looked inside with a feeling of triumph. None of these ingredients should ever have been in the same trolley, never mind the same plate. For once Nat felt ahead of the game. This revolting meal would see off Miss Hunny in no time and make sure she NEVER EVER CAME BACK.

CHAPTER NINE

• • • •

IT WAS FRIDAY MORNING AND NAT WAS IN HER FIRST lesson. It was quieter than usual because Darius had already been sent to sit outside the Head's office even BEFORE registration. Nat reckoned this must be a personal best.

With her gibbering friend gone, she couldn't cheat in maths any more, but something else rather wonderful happened to make up for it. Someone else sat next to her, someone she'd only managed to say hello to a few times, but thought might be nice. Someone NORMAL.

Penny Posnitch was a small, pretty girl with a dark brown bob and clear blue eyes that Nat was immediately jealous of. She always seemed to be happy and smiling, which made Nat wonder what it was Penny knew that she didn't. What would be so great about making friends with Penny was that Penny was exactly halfway up the class popularity ladder.

At the very top of the popularity ladder was a girl so amazing that everybody wanted to be her friend, despite the fact that she didn't appear to like anybody back. Flora Marling was tall and slim and had her ears pierced TWICE in both ears. She wore a bra and was said to have a boyfriend in Year 8. Her older sister was in a shampoo commercial. The whole class was convinced Flora Marling had a secret tattoo, she was THAT awesome.

Anyway, that was the top of the ladder, so far up that Nat wouldn't even dare try to be her friend. Right at the bottom of the popularity ladder was Darius. Other kids might move a few places up and down the ladder over time, but these two were already fixed at either end. Everyone knew that they were there for good.

But little smiling Penny was definitely halfway up, way higher than Nat but not quite out of reach. And now, here she was, sharing a desk with her! Nat tried to think of something to say to her as Mr Frantz droned on about adding x to y. She panicked briefly when she couldn't think of a single interesting thing about herself to say. Fortunately, Penny was a chatty creature and she went first.

"Do you like Princess Bo?" whispered Penny, who was drawing pictures inside her right-angled triangle. Nat guessed that was a pop star.

"Course," she fibbed. *It's not really a fib*, she told herself. *I probably will when I hear her. Which actually means I do like her.*

"I don't any more," said Penny.

Great, thought Nat, *this is going well*. But Penny was chatting on.

"Ever since I saw my dad dancing to her

new single. In the kitchen. In his boxer shorts, in front of Mum and everything. He'd been drinking *wine*. Can you imagine what that was like for me?"

"Did it make you want to find the biggest, deepest darkest cave in the universe and then get a digger to make it deeper and darker and then jump in it and get the digger to fill it up again on top of you?" asked Nat.

"Um… Something like that," said Penny, slightly alarmed.

"Well join the club. The last time my dad danced around to a pop record wasn't in the kitchen, it was in IKEA. Just after he put a sink plunger on his head and said he was a dalek."

"Oh – my – gosh," said Penny. "Well mine still sends me valentine cards with 'from your secret admirer brackets Dad' on."

"Mine puts my birthdays in the paper with PHOTOS."

They both squealed with shared horror, little toes curled inside their socks.

Penny lent Nat her third best ink pen and Nat thought this business of making friends might not be so hard, after all.

It was an unusually warm sunny day and maybe that's why everyone was in a good mood, but it could have been raining cats and dogs and Nat would have been happy. Break time whizzed by in a blur. Thanks to Penny, Nat met a whole bunch of OTHER GIRLS, like Abi Plummer who was the thirteenth fastest swimmer in the county, and Frankeee O'Riordan who spelled her name with three e's.

True, they were only sort of friendly, and kept asking Nat nervously where her weird friend Darius was, but Nat didn't care. By the time she went in for her geography lesson with Miss Austen, she was certain she'd cracked it. Finally, she was getting 'in'. And it felt great. Better yet, Darius had now been sent to pick up litter as he was clearly unable to sit outside the Head's office without doing handstands and Penny sat next to Nat AGAIN! Nat caught a glimpse of him outside through the window, shoving crisp packets in a big plastic bag. Guiltily she turned her head away. Towards her new friend Penny Posnitch.

It's true that Penny doesn't make me laugh as much as Darius, reasoned Nat, *but that's probably my fault. Look at Dad. He doesn't make me laugh either and he's funny for a living.* And though she had to admit she found Penny's constant babble about pop music and hair bands and TV soaps a tiny bit, well, boring, it didn't matter. She watched as Penny drew pictures of animals inside her volcano and decided to push these thoughts out of her head. The important thing was she was making the right sort of friend at last. She smiled at Penny, who wrinkled up her nose.

"Who's done that?" said Penny. "Has Darius come back in?"

Nat sniffed. There was a funny smell coming from somewhere. Funny, as in farty.

"She who smelt it, dealt it," Nat said without

thinking, before she could stop herself. She put her hand over her mouth. She'd been sitting next to Darius for too long.

"She who did the rhyme, committed the crime," countered Penny, who looked a bit upset.

Well, thought Nat, *if you're going to be like that.* "She who denied it, supplied it."

Penny looked genuinely hurt. Her lip trembled. Her eyes started looking a bit watery.

Uh-oh, thought Nat.

Darius would have continued that game pretty much all lesson, thought Nat, getting ruder and funnier. He was a poet of poo. So far, his greatest contribution to lavatory-based literature was the epic poem, *Diarrhoea*, now one hundred and six verses long. Obviously it's too rude and disgusting to print, but some of his more inventive rhymes were:

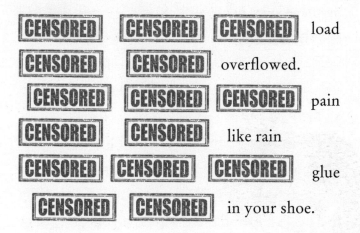 load

overflowed.

pain

like rain

glue

in your shoe.

Nathalia was still chuckling at this when she noticed Penny had her hand up.

"Please, miss, can I move, something really smells."

"It can't be that bad," said Miss Austen, coming over and sniffing. "Oh lord, it is – yes, sit by the window." Miss Austen cast a cold eye over Nathalia. "Do you need to be excused?" she asked in a whisper that was loud enough for everyone to hear.

Nat felt her cheeks burning. "It's not me," she said.

But the smell was getting worse. And it continued to get worse as the lesson dragged slowly on. By the time the class had finished colouring in their lava flows, her eyes were watering and everyone had moved their desks away from her.

It was only when Nat was sitting – on her own – at lunch that she discovered Dad's warm, smelly egg and cress sandwiches in her bag. The clingfilm had peeled off and there was now yolk and gunge sticking to all her books. She remembered with horror that she'd moaned about how rubbish school dinners were. Then she saw a little note next to the eggy mess. It read:

'Darling girl, I thought I'd surprise you.'

You did that, Dad – well done, she thought. The note went on:

'Hope these are nicer than your usual lunch. The eggs are organic so we need to use them up as they probably won't stay fresh for very long.'

Nat sighed and started scraping her English book clean.

"Oy, Buttface, what's that smell?" said Darius, barging in next to her. "She who coughed, cracked one off."

Nat sighed again. Back with Darius. Though she had to admit it was quite nice to see him, and just to make that totally clear, she rubbed egg in his hair.

In fact, she was so relieved to see him, all thoughts of Miss Hunny's visit that night went out of her head, right up until she went into her next lesson. Which was English – with Miss Hunny. Nat noticed coldly that she was wearing very different sorts of clothes to those she'd had on all week.

Normally Miss Hunny favoured frills and high collars and cardigans. Nat thought she usually looked like a receptionist, or a woman that worked in a chemist's shop. Or even an English teacher. But not today. Today she had on her 'going out for dinner with an old friend who I'm going to see lots and lots of in the future' outfit. She was wearing a fitted skirt and a pretty, lacy blouse. Nat didn't approve of teachers looking like ordinary people at the best of times. *They should let others know they are teachers,* she thought. So we can avoid them.

Miss Hunny gave Nathalia a big smile when she came in. A smile as if to say: "I'm here, I'm not going anywhere and I'm going to come to your house all the time and I'm going to find out all your little secrets and everyone in your class will think we're friends and, yes, this will basically ruin your life forever. Compare and contrast that, little girl."

It took Nat a while to realise what was different about this lesson but finally she worked it out. Darius wasn't sitting under the desk, or trying to eat his pencil case. In fact, she realised, Darius never sat under his desk or ate his pencil case in Miss Hunny's English class. And today, Darius was sitting exceptionally still, looking straight at Miss Hunny. When she came over to tell him to please stop writing his letter 'r's the wrong way round, she put a hand on his shoulder, and rather than just bite her as he normally would, Darius smiled. It was an odd smile and it took Nat a long time to realise why it was odd. He suddenly looked more like an ordinary boy and less like the deranged monster he usually resembled.

Nat decided she preferred him flicking bogeys at Dennis Skinner's head.

But she couldn't waste time puzzling over his strange behaviour. Time was running out and what if her menu from hell plan wasn't enough… Then, just before the end of the lesson, she came up with another GENIUS EVIL PLAN. *You are on a roll, Nathalia*, she thought. *You go girl.* And so when Miss Hunny came over to help Darius spell 'disembowel' in his 'What I did in my holidays' essay, Nat went for it while Darius gurned happily.

"Miss, you still coming round tonight?" she asked quietly. She didn't want anyone else to hear.

"That's the plan," Miss Hunny smiled.

"Only I've invited Darius. And he's definitely coming." She kicked Darius under the desk, but he wasn't paying her the slightest bit of attention.

"Oh," said her teacher, startled. "Well, that'll be – er – nice."

"Yeah, Dad says he's really looking forward to seeing him." *Again, not really a fib*, she thought. *It's the kind of stupid thing Dad WOULD say...*

"Did he?" She sounded doubtful. She looked at Darius, who was grinning stupidly.

"Didn't he tell you? Probably didn't think it was important."

Miss Hunny was silent for a moment. *This is it*, thought Nat. *This is where she thinks of an excuse not to come. Tonight she'll be washing her budgie/ decorating her fridge/ironing her cat/getting arrested, ANYTHING other than spending more time with Darius, the terror of 7H. But hang on*, thought Nat. The terror of 7H was now acting more like a teacher's pet than a classroom monster.

"How many esses in 'explode', miss?" he asked meekly.

Miss Hunny flicked a bit of egg out of his hair kindly.

"Maybe we can do an extra half an hour on this when I see you tonight," she said.

Nat put her head on her desk, hard.

Oh well, she thought, *at least I still have Dad's mash-up*. She almost told Miss Hunny to book next week off sick in advance.

"Where do you think you're going?" she said to Darius, as he followed her to the Atomic Dustbin. School had just ended and although he'd been back to his usual monkey-like self in Miss Eyre's tedious history class, it was all too late and she was still annoyed with him. He had been her last chance to stop her teacher coming round and he'd blown it by being nice. When was he ever nice?

"You invited me," he said. "Didn't you?"

His hands went in his pockets and he looked down at the ground. His scuffed shoes traced a rude word on the tarmac.

"Well…" Nat paused. "Won't you need to arrange it with your parents, though?"

"Oswald's not around this weekend," he said.

"So who's supposed to be looking after y—" Nat stopped. What did it matter? She caved in. "Oh, get in," she said, opening the van door and dodging a falling cricket bat. "Dad, Darius is coming for dinner tonight."

"Lovely," said Dad. "Hop in, whoever you are."

Darius hopped, and was suddenly covered in Dog.

"He likes you," said Dad, as Darius rolled around the floor, getting licked to within an inch of his life.

"I like him," said Darius. They spent the journey home under the table together, barking.

CHAPTER TEN

••••

WHY IS THIS FUNNY? WONDERED NATHALIA, as she vacuumed the kitchen. *Why am I giggling? It's only Darius doing a rubbish impression of a ghost. It's not even a good impression, as ghosts tend not to do robot dancing.* She giggled again.

I suppose he did make an effort with the costume, she thought. Darius *was* very white, thanks less to the magic of the supernatural and more to the magic of self-raising flour. Flour which was now all over the kitchen. But even though Darius was funny, Dad should be telling him off. Nathalia sighed and hoovered the Dog, who quite enjoyed licking flour from a kitchen floor. A proper dad would not join in with the dancing, either. He'd be shouting and stuff.

Nathalia was a bit uncertain what proper dad 'stuff' was, because she'd never seen it. But it wasn't this. Dad turned up the radio and did a poor quality moonwalk. Nat winced. It was only funny when Darius did it.

It was not long after Dad whipped out his bongos that Nat suddenly stopped tidying. It happened just like that – one second she was a blur of mop and flour and the next she was frozen in mid-clean. A strange calm came over her. She could no longer hear Dad's terrible hip-hop bongo beat, or Darius's alarming Bongo Rap. She smiled to herself as she realised something lovely and she chucked the mop on the floor where it lay with the rest of the stuff Dad and Darius had left lying about.

With a chuckle she walked upstairs to her room, threw herself on her bed with a magazine and waited. *This is perfect*, she thought. *There's no way that stupid, drippy Miss Hunny will stay five minutes in this madhouse.* She stretched out on her bed. *She probably won't even make it through the front door.* Nat started flicking through the brightly coloured pages of the magazine. *Dunno why I got Dad to buy me this*, she thought. *Utter rubbish. Look at it – dog, girl pop star smiling, kittens, boy pop star not smiling, dolphin, quiz:* Are you a dog, cat, dolphin or pop star? Nat yawned.

And all these rubbish problems. Problems about hair, teeth, boys, school bullies. Hah. Nothing about dads. I'll write in, she thought. *I'll tell them something.* She closed her eyes in the late afternoon sunlight. She dreamt of kittens playing the bongos. And dolphins squeaking surprisingly rude words.

The doorbell woke her with a start. For a second she couldn't recognise the feeling she'd woken up with. Then – ah yes, happiness. She ungummed her eyes and thought, *That'll be Miss Hunny. This'll be good.* She swung her legs over the side of the bed. *Better hurry*, she thought, *I don't want to miss seeing her run off screaming.* Coming down the stairs, Nat was disappointed not to hear either bad bongos or revolting rhymes. And the smell coming from the recently destroyed kitchen was actually… rather nice.

Oh, I get it – it's still a dream, she thought, and tried to fly down the last two steps. *I wonder where the dolphins have gone?*

Five minutes later she was lying flat on the sofa with a family-sized bag of frozen peas on her ankle and a family-sized scowl on her face.

"Ice, ice, ice," trilled Miss Hunny, applying the frozen veg to the tender area. She'd done a first-aid course and was now something of an expert. "I – C – E. The 'I' stands for ice, obviously, the 'C' for compression…" Here she squeezed the bag of peas tight, causing Nat to yelp. "And the 'E' stands for, let me think… 'E' for…"

"Electricity?" suggested Darius hopefully, eyeing up a socket.

"I've got some jump leads in the van," added Dad doubtfully.

"'E' for elevation, you morons," shouted Nat, lifting her leg above her head so high that all her change fell out of her pockets. Her bad mood wasn't because of the pain in her ankle. It was because she felt MASSIVELY CHEATED. Dad and Darius had sneakily hidden the bongos and tidied up everything. She couldn't for the life of her understand why Darius was being so nice.

Darius sat on the sofa and put her foot on his shoulder. "What are you doing?" she asked, suspicious. "Helping," he replied simply, casting a quick glance at Miss Hunny, who was now disappearing into the kitchen. He tore his eyes away and started picking his nose and playing with the TV remote. *I'm having that remote control sterilised tomorrow*, thought Nat. She would have said something out loud but a programme came on that she liked and she forgot what she was about to say.

"Your daughter does like being the centre of attention," murmured Miss Hunny to Dad as they all sat down to eat. She said it quietly but Nat had bat ears when she wanted to and she glowered at her teacher. She was going to say something rude or 'accidentally' jab her with a fork but then she realised that this would make her the centre of attention again and Miss Hunny would be proved right! *You're clever*, she thought darkly. *You are a worthy opponent.*

She expected Dad to defend her but Dad wasn't really listening. He was struggling to unscrew the cap on a bottle of wine Miss Hunny had just brought. "Remember when we were students?" he laughed, finally pouring them a glass. "You always used to bring round that horrible wine from Uzbekistan or somewhere that cost about four pence a gallon and we couldn't let it spill on the kitchen table in case it took all the Formica off and— oh."

Dad had finally clocked the bottle's familiar Uzbekistan label. And the look on Miss Hunny's face.

"Well I've missed it!" He took a sip. His eyes started to water. "Yum. Wait, let me get you a coaster for your glass."

"Dad doesn't even like wine, he likes beer," grumbled Nat to Darius.

"My brother Oswald's not picky," replied Darius. "He just likes getting drunk."

Nat looked at Darius, wondering if he was joking. She'd never seen Dad drunk. No, actually, there was that time on holiday when he fell into the hotel pool one night, but he'd said that was something he ate.

Anyway, Mum and Nat always took Dad's beer away long before he had the chance to really make a fool of himself. Thing is, after a couple of bottles of Olde Crotchpyce or whatever, Dad would tend to get very silly. He'd cuddle them both and say things like they were the best girls in the world, and that he wanted to hug them and NEVER LET GO.

At which point Mum would put the kettle on and make him drink coffee until he apologised. But, Nat realised with a shudder, Mum wasn't there tonight. Icy fingers grabbed at her throat, crawling down her back and... actually, it was only Darius chucking peas at her so she kicked him off.

"Where is Emma? I'm sorry not to see her," said Miss Hunny.

"She sends her love. She's away all week doing this big new job," said Dad proudly.

"She was always going to do well," said Miss Hunny. "She even made money when we were students. What is it she's doing now?"

Dad's eyes glazed over. "We-ell," he bluffed, "it's a bit complicated."

Miss Hunny gave a sort of laugh. "I know I'm just an ordinary English teacher at a VERY ordinary school – no offence, children – but I'll probably understand."

But Nat knew very well that Dad had no idea what Mum did for a living because business just confused him.

"She does things with stuff," he said eventually.

"Go on..."

"Oooh, we had some fun at college, the three of us, didn't we?" said Dad, changing the subject rapidly. "The stories we could tell you, Nat..."

Please don't, thought Nat dryly. The very worst thing about Dad after he'd had even ONE drink was that he loved telling stories. And generally he liked telling stories about... she could hardly bring herself to think it... he liked telling stories about... HER.

Dad took a big swig of wine, coughed and said, "But better than that, I've got some really funny stories about Nathalia."

Noooooo...

Now, according to Dad, the top five 'really funny' Nat stories (so far) are:

The one where she gets that rash shaped like a Pokemon.

The one where she gets stuck in a ball pit.

The one where she's filmed singing, aged four, on her new karaoke machine. Singing, and taking her clothes off.

The one where she's car sick down the back of Dad's head.

The one where Dad's car sick down the back of *her* head.

Nat looked to Darius to do something evil, dangerous, weird, smelly, and/or insane to distract Dad. She knew he could do it; he could be all those things for eight school hours, without a lunch break. But oh no. Today here he was, sitting still and trying to smooth his hair down. What WAS the matter with him?

"Did I ever tell you the story about Nathalia and the dog biscuits?"

That doesn't even make the top five, thought

Nat, helplessly. *Dad's going for the whole top twenty. This is terrible. It cannot get worse.*

And then the doorbell rang.

CHAPTER ELEVEN

· · · ·

"Cooooee, only me," said Bad News Nan, walking straight past Dad with two shopping bags. "Oooh, is it dinner time? Lovely. You'll never guess who's just been hit by a bus." She paused for a microsecond, sitting down and noticing Miss Hunny. "Ivor, introduce me. He's terrible, my son. You'd think he'd been dragged up. I blame the bang on the back of his head when he got dropped as a baby. Well, he was born bright yellow, it's no wonder the nurse dropped him."

Saved, thought Nat, and dived on her nan's large lap.

"What's for dinner? I could eat a morsel – my stomach thinks my throat's been cut. I've brought some biscuits for afters. They were only a pound at Everything's a Pound. Not that I should shop there after what happened to Mr Hanoomansingh in the dry goods section. It's his wife I feel sorry for. And the people who had to clean it up."

"Hello, Mum," said Dad, as Bad News Nan paused for breath. "This is a surprise."

"You'd think he'd say *nice* surprise, wouldn't you, dear?" she continued, adding to Nat's joy, "but that's him all over. He's never been grateful. He won a scooter in a beautiful baby competition when he was three but would he play with it? He would not. Just because it was pink."

"No, it was because you entered me in the girls' section."

"Well, you were a pretty child. You'd never have won in the boys', have some sense. Oh, but he's never had much sense. I could tell you some stories, missy."

Miss Hunny smiled politely. "Please don't," she said.

"Please do," said Nat.

"I wouldn't embarrass him," said Bad News Nan. "Not that he didn't embarrass me. Like the time he threw a tantrum in the toy shop because they'd sold out of mutant turtles."

"It was my birthday, and you'd promised," muttered Dad.

"I said this is no way for a fourteen-year-old to behave. I dragged him out by his ear, I admit it. I know these days parents can be locked up for less, but that's why you can't go out at night any more. Teenagers running riot, with hoods on; s'awful. I want to know who sells them these hoods, that's what I want to know. You're not safe in your own street. I blame the schools. Teaching's gone right down the pan. Let me tell you…"

Miss Hunny's lips tightened as Bad News Nan told her. "I'll get you a plate," said Nat happily.

She skipped into the kitchen, pain in her ankle a distant memory. This was going to be the greatest night of her life.

Even before the meal was finished, Dad was looking decidedly green round the edges. They'd already been treated to some choice nuggets from his childhood, from his fear of iceberg lettuce to how he once superglued Nan to a caravan toilet in Rhyl (Darius's personal favourite).

Nat wasn't bothered that Dad had played it safe with the cooking and bought a big frozen lasagne. She had an hour of joy at the dinner table as Bad News Nan went on and on and on. She never ran out of anything to say for two very good reasons. Firstly, she repeated everything about six times, just to make sure everyone had heard it. And secondly, if she couldn't remember the end to a story, she JUST MADE IT UP. If she got really stuck she'd nick ideas from soaps or daytime telly or films. Miss Hunny might well have been surprised that Dad had foiled a bank robbery, hitched round the world and had an evil twin called Colin, but she didn't show it. She was still too annoyed at Bad News Nan's opinions of teachers.

And even Darius isn't safe tonight, Nat thought gleefully, as Bad News Nan got him in a headlock, spat on her hanky and wiped tomato sauce off his face. He struggled helplessly in her mighty bosom, but THERE WAS NO ESCAPE.

Bad News Nan was actually called Glenys, but she seemed to collect terrible hard-luck stories the way other people collect stamps, or the way Darius collected detentions. People just told her this stuff. They couldn't help themselves; she was a bad-news magnet and just sucked it out of them. If you wanted to know who was in trouble, or had lost their job, or had been eaten by an escaped bear, Bad News Nan would tell you. In fact, she'd tell you even when you didn't want to know.

And now she was telling them about Mr Karahan, from down at the kebab shop. Apparently he was suffering from pustules, the description of which had put them all off their trifle. Except Darius, who thought Nan was awesome, even if he was due another faceful of spitty Nan-hankie.

Hundreds of years ago, people believed in a thing called the wheel of fortune. It's really not complicated, so pay attention. Basically it says that when you are at the bottom, when your dog's been run over and you've come last in maths and you've been given a jumper for your birthday rather than an iPad, well, there's good news. One day the wheel will lift you up. You'll have more dogs and maths GCSEs and iPads than you'll know what to do with. You'll be on top!

Which is very nice.

However, remember this is a wheel, not a lift. If you are at the top, the only way is down, loser.

This belief – that no matter how happy you are, you'll soon be doomed – is one of the reasons why people in the Middle Ages were really miserable. Well, that and the Black Death. Oh and the constant wars, poverty, filth, lack of due legal process and a really long wait for the TV to come on. Bad News Nan was born 500 years too late. She'd have loved it.

Anyway, Nat, currently sat at the top of the wheel, felt a slight waver. Bad News Nan had got a fruit pip under her top plate and had taken it out to scrape it with her hanky. A scrubbed Darius watched with horror as he realised SHE

ONLY HAD ONE HANKY.

Worse than this, Miss Hunny finally got an opportunity to speak.

"There'savacancyforsomeonetochairthe POGSschoolcommitteeandyou'dbeperfect," she gabbled, trying to fit as many words in as possible before Nan put her teeth back in.

"Sorry,didn'tcatchthat," gabbled Dad.

Nat felt the wheel tilt downwards sharply.

"She said there's a vacancy for some idiot to chair the stupid POGS school committee, whatever that is, and you're the idiot," said Darius automatically, without thinking, or taking his eyes of Nan, scrubbing, scrubbing.

"Oh, I'd love to get more involved in Nathalia's school," said Dad.

Nat's wheel was picking up speed. Downwards.

"I've split me plate," said Nan.

"POGS stands for our new Parents Organising Group Scheme. They run all sorts of fun events. You know – school outings, discos, oh, and we'd like to get in one of those really cool theatre companies that do Shakespeare in rap, really connect with the kids."

Nan toyed with her top set. "I thought it was weakened when I caught the Dog chewing it," she said, tutting.

Miss Hunny finished the Uzbek red in one gulp and soldiered on. "With your energy, and the way you connect with children, and all your contacts in the media, you'd be perfect. What do you say? Can I put your name forward?"

Nat knew her wheel had hit rock bottom before she even heard Dad say yes.

As it turned out, Nat was wrong. Much later, when the bouncing Darius had finally been forcibly detained in the spare room, and Bad News Nan was snoring in the armchair in the living room, Nat did something sneaky. She crept downstairs in her PJs to 'get a glass of water', which actually meant 'to listen to Dad and Miss Hunny without them knowing'.

She heard Miss Hunny saying quietly,

"...yes, I think he's charming, and I think he's hiding a very good brain in there, but most of the teachers disagree with me. They want Darius moved. He's a bad influence on Nathalia's class."

"But won't he be a bad influence on the other class?" asked Dad.

Miss Hunny frowned. Nat couldn't actually see her face, as she was peeking through a crack in the door, but her voice *sounded* frowny. "The school have made a new class. For kids who are ALL bad influences."

Nat knew the one she meant. It was the class that all the other kids hurried past.

"The school's not so worried about them," her teacher continued. "I think most teachers just want them to get to Year Eleven without burning the place down."

Miss Hunny sighed unhappily.

Nathalia found herself wishing Miss Hunny wasn't Dad's friend because, in that moment, looking at her kind face, she rather liked her.

"It doesn't seem very fair to Darius," said Dad.

Miss Hunny didn't reply.

It doesn't seem very fair to ME either, thought Nat, stomping back upstairs, her fake glass of water forgotten. *I've only got one friend, even if he is a bad influence. And calls me Buttface. And eats his own bogeys. And farts the first three bars of* 'Frére Jacques' *in French – OK, that one's actually funny.*

Hang on, said the little Evil Villain inside Nat, *without Darius you could have proper friends like Penny and Abi and Frankeee with three e's.* Nat was tempted but then peeked in on the terror of 7H. He was curled up on the floor, fast asleep, cuddling the Dog.

CHAPTER TWELVE

....

IT WAS ONLY DAYS AFTER THE DREADED DINNER and Nat already hated POGS more than double games. Which she was now doing. It was drizzling, of course.

"All I hear is POGS POGS *POGS*," she gasped to Darius as they jogged round the playing field. They were both being punished for something or other that was probably Darius's fault.

"What?" said Darius. "Hold on, I've got to stop running. I think my breakfast is coming back." There was a horrible noise. Nat looked away. "I don't remember eating that," said Darius, wiping his face with a torn sleeve. "In fact, I don't remember eating breakfast." They jogged on. "Right, what stupid things were you saying?" continued Darius. "Ow, stop pinching."

"Dad and his rubbish committee," she complained. A well-hit rounders ball landed at her feet and she kicked it savagely into some bushes. *Hope it lands in the sick*, she thought.

"What committee?" said Darius, cartwheeling.

"Don't you ever listen?" said Nat in her best Mum voice. "My dad's now running this school thing with teachers and parents and they want to make up rubbish things for us to do. Boring trips and stupid competitions and boot fairs and jumble sales and talent shows and who knows what else. He wants to interfere with EVERYTHING. He watched a documentary on food the other day and now he's trying to take turkey twizzlers off school dinners."

"I don't want to talk about school dinners," said Darius, still a bit green.

"He's even trying to organise a 'Bring your dad to school day'." Darius shrugged.

Nat went on, "Which I'm not doing – he's at this school more than me anyway."

This was all such terrible news, she couldn't see why Darius didn't care. At least on her behalf.

"Bo-ring," said Darius, who was now crawling into a bush on his stomach, holding an invisible rifle. "Let's play snipers." *Oh well*, Nat told herself, *as long as Dad doesn't organise a disco, it might not be too bad.*

Soon the little skipping figure of Penny Posnitch appeared. Nat smiled – she reckoned Penny was ALMOST a friend now. There was just one thing in the way and it was currently in a bush somewhere. But even though Evil Villain Nat still nagged her that she'd be better off without him, Good Nat still didn't want him to get sent to that horrible class. She sighed; life was complicated.

"Miss Eyre says you can come back now," said Penny. "Because I said that you said you were sorry and wouldn't do it again."

"Thanks," said Nat, thinking, *But I'm not and I will.*

"And I fibbed and said you were our best player." Penny stopped and looked round nervously. "Where's HE gone?"

No one liked to say Darius's name. It was considered unlucky.

"Oh, he's in a bush," said Nat.

"Think he'll come out?"

"You can never tell."

Nat walked back to the match with Penny. "Did you really say I was your best player?" she asked happily.

What happened five minutes later takes some explaining. This is the true version of events that Mrs Trout the Head refused to listen to.

It was Nat's turn to bat. The girl standing behind her was on the opposite team. Nat didn't like her much, and wasn't going to make the effort to like her because this girl wasn't very popular either. This girl had decided that she was going to make herself more popular by teasing Nat. So, when the first ball was thrown, she shouted,

"Where's your pet dog?"

Swish. Nat missed. She thought about the question, puzzled. Her pet Dog was at home, barking at people wearing hats. He hated hats. But there was something nasty in the tone of the question. From out of the corner of her eye she saw Darius wander up with twigs in his hair.

"Look, here he is," the girl said, laughing unpleasantly. A few other girls joined in.

"Hey," said Nat, annoyed, turning round just as the second ball was thrown at her. It hit her on the back of the head.

"Watch it," said Nat, spinning round, really annoyed now.

"Will you pay attention, Nathalia," scolded Miss Eyre. "Foul ball."

"Was not," argued the bowler.

"Don't argue. There are still two balls left," insisted Miss Eyre. The bowler scowled and drew her arm back as far as she could. Nat gripped her bat tight.

"Thinks she's special just cos her dad's always coming to school."

"Stop being mean," warned Nat, turning round again. The ball smacked her on the head even harder.

"*That* ball was good," said Miss Eyre.

"Why?" shouted Nat. "It hit me in the same place."

"Stop jumping around, Nathalia, and get on with the game. Last ball. If you miss this, you're out and you lose the game."

Nat narrowed her eyes and stared at the bowler. The bowler put the wooden ball behind her back, turning it with her fingers. *She's going to try and spin this*, thought Nat. *It's going to go to my left, I can feel it.*

A little breeze tickled Nat's face and she made tiny movements with her feet, adjusting. She breathed in and held the breath, planning to breathe out the moment she made contact with the ball. Maybe she *could* be their best player. Yeah, this rotten ball was going to go miles. If she hit it hard enough, she reckoned she could bounce it off Miss Eyre's car and dent it. Everything was quiet.

"Daddy's girl, Daddy's girl," said the girl behind her. Five seconds later Nat was chasing after her with the bat.

"Thanks for taking out that Tracey Lucas," said Nat to Darius, as they sat outside the Head's office awaiting their fate. "She was sitting on my head for so long I'm still picking bits of grass out of my teeth. I don't think she was knocked out *too* badly, do you?"

Darius shrugged.

"You do understand you have to tell Mrs Trout that it was someone else's fault, it was an accident and that you weren't even there, in that order?" Darius looked blankly at her.

"Do you WANT to get sent to that horrible class?" she said angrily. But he just rubbed his scuffed shoes together and picked at a hole in his jumper.

"Stuff happens," he said finally. Nat gave up. She put her ear to the door of the office for a quick listen.

Inside, the Head was telling Dad about what had happened. Nat only heard every other word but then so did Dad, because he never paid attention. What they both heard was this: *Darius... Nathalia... broken... bleeding... not acceptable... unruly... language... shocking... in all my years I've never... ashamed of themselves... leaving me no choice... last chance and must try harder.*

Then after a few quiet moments in which Nat imagined Dad was probably nodding gravely and pretending he had been listening, she heard him say, "Did I tell you about the trip we're organising to the theme park?"

"Is that really suitable for the children?" replied the Head. "We're having enough trouble calming the little swi— Ahem, the little *angels* down. Sounds like too much fun to me. Exciting them is the last thing we need."

"Well, some fool suggested we go brass rubbing..." Nat heard him say, wincing, wondering if round about now Dad was noticing the enormous brass rubbings hanging proudly on the wall of the Head's office.

A few moments later Dad emerged. He winked at the two children in the way other naughty children do when they've got away with something.

"Cheer up, you two," he said. "You've only got the one week of detentions. And then next week we're all going to the cathedral to do some brass rubbings. Won't that be – um – fun?"

"No," said Nat.

She was right. It wasn't fun. But at least no one had to do any brass rubbings. They were all chucked out of the cathedral long before they got their paper and chalks out.

CHAPTER THIRTEEEN

. . . .

TRY AS SHE MIGHT, NAT COULDN'T MAKE MUM understand the horror of Dad taking her on a school trip. In front of girls who were ever so much very nearly her friends.

In fact, she had a horrible feeling that Mum thought it was actually funny. It was the way Mum kept a very straight face when she said things like, "Won't it be great to have your whole class see just how lucky we are to have your father in our lives."

Nat knew it was hopeless trying to talk Dad

out of it; he was super-keen to get involved. He even bought a book on the history of the rubbish cathedral AND one called Brass Rubbing for Utter Morons or something.

The big trip did not start well. And that was the best it got. Dad had originally booked the coach to take them to the amusement park and of course had forgotten to tell the coach driver about the change of plan. So initially they pulled up at the Super Happy Funtime Land of Excitement, and the thirty kids on the coach stopped eating sweets and playing Nintendo and texting and fighting and being sick in crisp packets long enough to give a massive cheer. Which was almost as loud as the massive BOO they gave when Dad told the coach driver to turn round.

To be fair to the children, the majority of the bad language came from the driver, a certain Brian Futtock, from Futtocks Coach Hire and Pest Control.

Futtocks weren't the school's normal coach

service, but they were much cheaper and Dad had wanted to keep the costs down. It was fast becoming clear why exactly they were so cheap – the coach was awful. It was old and noisy and smelt of rat wee. Just like the driver.

Nat could hear Dad trying to make conversation at the front of the bus. "It's an unusual business, coach hire and rat catching," he was saying, clearly trying to ignore the food fight that had broken out on the back seat, and the glare of his daughter's icy gaze, boring into the back of his head, and the bits of screwed-up paper that occasionally bounced off the back of *her* head, and Darius trying to stuff an entire packet of skittles up his nose for a 5p bet.

But Brian Futtock clearly didn't feel like talking. He just grunted, not taking his eyes from the road.

He had a face full of boils and a long nose with hairs sprouting from his nostrils, like whiskers. Nat guessed he just drove round in a coach all day with a boot full of rat traps and a hammer.

She guessed right.

Finally they pulled up at the coach park near the cathedral. As the kids spilled out Nat noticed Dad doing a quick head count.

"You're supposed to do that BEFORE they get on the coach," said Nat. "You are rubbish."

"Thirty," said Dad smugly. "See? That's everyone."

"Except Miss Eyre," said Nat. "You've left her behind."

"Oh," said Dad. He checked his mobile. It was off. When he turned it on he had thirty-five missed calls and eight rude texts, all from Miss Eyre.

Nat had realised Dad had forgotten Miss Eyre when they pulled out of the school gates, but hadn't reminded him on purpose.

"Well," she said happily, "I don't suppose we can do the visit now – what a shame; let's go back to school. See you at teatime, Dad."

"No, we're here now and we're already late," said Dad, deleting texts like mad. "Let's go, everyone, this way!"

"You can't take us out on your own, it's ILLEGAL," said Nat, her feet planted like a miniature policewoman. "We'll have to go home."

"I'm sure I can keep you lot in order," said Dad, sounding unsure. "Can you tell Darius to stop asking passers-by for money? He is not working for Save the Whale."

"I'm not doing your dirty work," said Nat. "You're on your own."

The coach started pulling away. "Where are you going?" shouted Dad, running after it.

"Rats," said Brian Futtock, head out of the driver's window.

"I'll cancel your cheque if you don't come back right now," said Dad, getting out of breath.

"Outbreak of big black ones. It's an emergency. I'll be back at three. Four at the latest." And with that, the coach sped off in the direction of a rat and kid-free pub.

Dad sighed, made Darius hand back the ten-pound note he'd swindled out of a nice old lady in a knitted hat, and ushered the swarm of kids inside the cathedral. They all stopped just beyond the enormous carved wooden doors. The cathedral was huge and cool, sweet-smelling and very, very quiet. There was a low, echoing murmur of people inside that quietened the children, but not for very long.

Dad had already got into his first row. And they were only at the entrance.

"What do you mean, 'admission fee'?" he said, outraged. "We should not have to pay to enter a house of the Lord." He sounded like the Archbishop of Canterbury. Nat winced. Dad only went to church on Christmas Eve because he liked carols and no one let him sing because he sounded horrible.

"It's a house of the Lord with a leaky roof," said The Guide. "And besides, school parties need a guide. Which is me. Which is twenty quid."

"I don't need a guide. I know about this cathedral," fibbed Dad, getting his wallet out nonetheless. Nat was surprised. She rarely saw Dad's wallet. "It's like an eclipse," Nat quipped to Darius. "You don't get to see it much." She was rather pleased with her gag.

"Transit of Venus" would be a better joke," said Darius, idly scratching his initials on the door with his little knife, "because it's rarer."

Nat snatched his knife off him, annoyed.

"You are aware of course that money is the root of all evil?" continued Dad loudly, as they began their tour. Dad rather liked money, except when he was handing it over. Nat cringed. This was going to be worse than she imagined. Within five minutes she had changed her mind. It was going to be A LOT worse than she imagined.

"You don't have to come in here, you know," said The Guide. She was a middle-aged woman, rather square, with a severe bob. "There's an arcade nearby." Thirty kids cheered. "Will you keep them quiet," she barked. Her words echoed around the high stone walls and shivered the stained glass.

She lowered her voice. "And there's a wedding today at the high altar. See if you can show some respect." Nat looked. Sure enough, in the hazy, stained-glass light, she saw a small wedding party at the far end of the cathedral. The vicar doing the service looked up at the group and The Guide mouthed, "Sorry."

"The cathedral's foundations were laid in 1235," said Dad loudly, guidebook in hand.

"I was going to say that," said The Guide, offended.

"Well you didn't, you were too busy drumming up business for the arcade," said Dad. Nat realised with alarm that The Guide was, to Dad, SOMEONE IN AUTHORITY. She knew where this generally led and wondered if anyone would notice if she snuck off and joined the wedding. *Maybe*, she thought wildly, *I could pretend to be a bridesmaid. How bad could that be?*

Darius was way ahead of her. "Weddings are ace. There'll be a party, and cake," he said, dragging her towards the high altar. "I went to my cousin's wedding. Before the police got there, there was loads of cake."

Behind her, Nat could hear The Guide and Dad rowing again, getting louder all the time.

"Bishop Odo's heart is NOT buried here," argued Dad. "I saw a documentary." They were standing next to a tombstone. The kids had stopped looking for brass things to rub and were all looking at Dad. This was far more interesting.

"What is buried here then?" asked one.

"His GIBLETS," said Dad. The class squealed in delight and disgust. "They only said heart because it sounds better than giblets."

"Are you allowed to be out with children?" said The Guide, angrily.

"I don't believe in telling them lies."

"Some lies are good for them."

"GIBLETS, GIBLETS," shouted the kids.

"What lies are good for children?" said Dad.

"We want giblets, show us the giblets."

"Oh, I don't know…" The Guide looked

around for inspiration. "Doggie heaven. That's rubbish for a start."

The children went silent.

Dad looked at The Guide. "Don't say that, they might hear you," he hissed, before announcing loudly, "Of course there's doggie heaven."

But The Guide just laughed nastily. "Oh, but you like the truth, don't you? So let's be one hundred per cent truthful to the little children, shall we?" she said. "Are you ready, kids? There – is – no – doggie – heaven."

There was a horrible silence. For about three seconds. Then...

Samantha Symons started wailing. "Buster's in doggie heaven. He *is*. Mummy promised. Waaaaaah."

"Look what you've done, you big meanie," said Dad.

"Giblets, giblets..." chanted the doggie-less kids who couldn't care less about doggie heaven.

"Waaah," went the doggie owners. Nat noticed Penny Posnitch was looking a bit wobbly-lipped too. Nat went over to her. "I can get Darius to do something horrible to her if you like," she whispered kindly.

The noise was awful. Over by the wedding, the vicar had just got to the bit where he asks if anyone has a good reason why Barry shouldn't marry Tiffany.

"Did someone say giblets?" he said. "And what's doggie heaven got to do with it?"

Darius gave a massive shout of glee. Nat tried to hide under a pew. Two little bridesmaids who had puppies burst into tears. The vicar shook his fist at Dad and the bride's mother jumped up and headed towards him, with fury burning in her eyes.

"I think you should go now," hissed The Guide. Dad was about to say something back when he noticed the bride's mother was holding a large umbrella with a spike on the tip and decided enough was enough.

"Follow me to the arcade, kids," he shouted. And ran.

"You can't let this lot loose in the arcade," said Nat, when they were all safely in the street outside. "You'll get us all expelled."

"I just said that to get everyone's attention," said Dad. "This will do." They were next to a small café. It smelt of old chip fat. A brownish kebab rotated slowly in the window. Dad saw Nat's face. "What?" he said. "Come on, I bet it's nicer than it looks."

"It couldn't be much worse..." replied Nathalia.

"We can't get back on the coach for hours. We'll stay here and I'll call for backup."

"You're not in the police force, Dad."

"It feels like the riot squad at the moment, love. Right, everyone, in here!"

The kids all piled into the empty caff. The owner put out his cigarette, wiped his greasy hands on his apron and worked out how much thirty kebabs would come to. He smiled.

"Now, listen, everyone, you can only order drinks," shouted Dad, as the rain came down outside. The café owner listened to the rain and doubled the price of his Cokes.

Two minutes later Dad admitted three things to Nat, each worse than the other.

First, half the kids were tucking into large plates of chips. The other half weren't. No, they were eating ice creams. This was going to cost him a FORTUNE.

Second, he'd lost his wallet.

Third, he'd lost Darius.

"I thought you were looking after him," said Dad, as they ran back to the cathedral.

"He's not my pet dog," panted Nat, keeping up, remembering guiltily where she'd last heard that expression, and feeling bad for walking off and leaving him.

"Think, Nat," he said. "Where did you see him last? What was Darius doing?"

"Fidgeting, burping, sitting upside down, the usual."

But Dad didn't seem to care. He was looking

at a small crowd of people, dressed for a wedding, standing around outside the cathedral, looking upwards at the huge spire, and pointing. A small figure was up on the roof, his little bare bum mooning the whole town.

"We found Darius then," said Nat.

The vicar, the bride and groom and The Guide were all looking especially furious.

"Wait here," said Dad, and went inside to face the wrath of God.

CHAPTER FOURTEEN

• • • •

OBVIOUSLY DAD GOT AWAY WITH IT. MUM CLEVERLY told him to make a donation to the Cathedral Roof Fund, so they'd drop the charges. And then Dad promised the Head a signed photo of Kerri, Bonehead and Cabbage, the local DJs, for her grand-daughter. Nat caught Dad forging their signatures one night soon after.

"Wouldn't they do it for you, love?" asked Mum, who had come home early and bought a huge Chinese takeaway with her. Nat could see Dad looked quite hurt, even though his face was stuffed with noodles.

"They said they're a bit too busy," he muttered. Mum sighed and Nat felt a twinge of loyalty for him.

"Maybe you *should* give them a prank call," said Nat. "Serve them right."

Dad ruffled her hair the way he did the Dog's fur. "Maybe," he said, "but I can't annoy them too much because I promised the Head they'd come and help me do a school disco."

So Dad was trying to organise a disco? Noooo. Nat's crispy won tons suddenly tasted like fear.

As for Darius... "You've missed that crisp packet," said the be-vested Mr MacAnuff, pointing at a little bag floating along the running track. Darius set off after it. It blew on to the playground where the other kids were enjoying their break as normal. Nat, who was hovering around Penny, Abi and three–e Frankeee, who were now *almost* talking to her, caught it and walked over to him.

"How much longer will you have to pick up

litter?" she said. "It's been ages now." *Ages of really boring breaks*, she might have added, but didn't want to admit it.

Darius shrugged. After his bare-faced (or rather bare-bottomed) cheek on the cathedral roof, he'd been on permanent litter duty. Most of this time had been spent looking after Mr MacAnuff's pride and joy, THE LAWN.

The Lawn was at the far end of the playing fields and was Mr MacAnuff's baby. It was green and flat and smooth, and glistened like a squashed frog. The Lawn was pampered and fed and nurtured like a favourite pet. The Lawn was perfect. It had been grown, years ago, from grass Mr MacAnuff dug up one night from his favourite football team's pitch. Two days later their star striker broke his ankle tripping over a big hole in their pitch, and without him, Mr MacAnuff's team got relegated. Mr MacAnuff thought it was worth the sacrifice. No one was ever allowed to walk on it. Every term he tried to ban pupils from LOOKING at it.

Mr MacAnuff shouted over to Darius. "That's enough chatting, Bagley. It's the open evening tomorrow – this place needs to be spotless for the parents." Darius sighed, chucked the crisp packet in the back of Nat's parka hood, and wandered off. "See you later, Buttface."

But Nat wasn't listening. She had a nasty sensation – open evening, parents, tomorrow. Had she forgotten something?

Halfway through maths that afternoon she remembered. "Aaargh!" she shouted in panic, making Mr Frantz drop his calculator, and Darius jab himself with a compass.

"I'm so dead," Nat wailed when she got home. Dad's face was dusty and he seemed a bit stiff after what he said was his latest bit of 'research' for a newspaper article – helping his mate Monkey Dave do some removals. She gabbled her woes to him nonetheless. "It's the stupid open evening at school tomorrow and everyone has to do a picture for the display, or else you get into trouble and I can't get into any more trouble."

"They haven't given you much time to do it in," said Dad.

"Well, they might have told us ages ago. I was going to do it during my breaks but –" she paused – "I haven't had time." This was vague, but true. She'd spent her breaks either trying to make friends or trying to make more litter for Darius to pick up (partly because it was fun and partly to keep him out of the way while she was trying to make new friends).

"How long have you had to do it?"

"That's not the point," she said. "The point is, I'm rubbish at drawing and it needs to be coloured in and I don't even think we've got any paints anyway and I'm really tired and can I go off sick tomorrow?"

Her lip was trembling.

"Oh, now don't upset yourself," said Dad. "I'll dig out some paper and glitter and glue and stuff, and there's some dried spaghetti here if you want to make a collage, and there're some tins of old paint in the van. You can do it. I'm sure you're not that bad."

An hour later, Nat was in bed, sobbing, and Dad was scraping up a hideous mess of paint and glitter and glue and pasta from the kitchen table. "No, I really am that bad," she yelled, before stomping off. *Stupid art, stupid open evening, stupid DAD*, thought Nat as she went to sleep in a massive huff.

"OMG, Dad, it's perfect," said Nat the next morning as she shovelled down her breakfast cereal. Nat was looking at a picture propped up on the kitchen table. Dad had got dark circles under his eyes.

"It's good enough to hand in, but still rubbish enough that it doesn't look like a grown-up did it for me. What a great idea. How did you do that?"

Dad smiled weakly and poured himself another cup of coffee. He looked tired, Nat thought guiltily, like he'd been up all night.

"You've even coloured it in and kept inside the lines and everything. But why have you drawn me with a pig?" Nat asked.

"It's the Dog," said Dad defensively.

"No, it's not," laughed Nat. "It's definitely a tiny pig."

"Do you want this picture or not?" asked Dad, a little bit irritably.

"Yeah, course," said Nat, signing her name on the picture. "I've just got to think of some reason why I'm playing with a little pig."

"Right, that's it," said Dad, grabbing the picture, "you can't have it now."

"Sorry, sorry, soz," said Nat, laughing and trying to snatch it back. She chased Dad around the kitchen, him waving it above his head. "I like pigs, honestly. I'll tell Miss Eyre that I want to be a vet."

"Tell me it looks like the Dog and you can have it back."

By now Nat was laughing so hard she could

barely get the words out. "I would, Dad, but you told me never to lie."

Dad picked her up and spun her round until she squealed. "See?" he said. "You think your daft old Dad can't do anything right."

"That is true, Dad," she said. "Except…" she giggled as he tickled her. "Not really, Dad. For once you have actually done something right. This is perfect."

Then she added the fatal words, "Nothing can go wrong."

Even as she said it, a little voice in her head was shouting, "Don't say it." But it was too late…

But for most of the day, Nat was proved right. The picture was a great success. Even Miss Eyre liked it. She liked it so much she took it to Mrs Trout. Nathalia stood there innocently as the Head admired Dad's effort.

But then Miss Eyre muttered evilly about how this proved that keeping Nat away from The Bagley at breaks was good for her. "Imagine how good it would be for her if he was – somewhere else," she added, meaning the naughty class. Nat wanted to kick her.

Miss Hunny, bringing the Head a lukewarm cup of something from the coffee machine that was either coffee or oxtail soup, overheard this and sent Nat out, where she was forced to listen through the keyhole.

"We agreed that the litter punishment was quite enough for Darius," said Miss Hunny. Miss Eyre said something about not thinking it was enough but the Head ignored her. "You seem to like this Bagley boy," she said to Miss Hunny. "I hope he's worth it."

Nat frowned. Why was this wretched Hunny woman so flipping *nice*?

Then they all went and put the picture in pride of place by the school entrance, ready for the open evening.

"The pig's very good," said Miss Eyre, squinting at the picture.

"I think she wants to be a vet," replied Mrs

Trout, talking as if Nat wasn't there.

"That explains why she hangs out with The Bagley," said Miss Eyre. "Vet practice." She realised Darius had appeared out of nowhere, still hunting litter. "Why are you here?"

"Everyone's gotta be somewhere," he said.

"I despair," said the Head, walking away. "I do, honestly."

As the teachers trotted off, Penny Posnitch went by, singing to herself. Nat thought Penny's picture was really brilliant. It was much better than Dad's, even if it was a bit silly – it was a picture of unicorns and fairies in a beautiful garden. Nat thought the fairies looked real enough to squish. (She hated fairies.)

"Yours is way better than mine," admitted Nat as Penny passed. "It should be at the entrance."

"Miss Eyre doesn't believe I did it on my own," said Penny lightly. "Just cos my dad's a painter she thinks I cheated and got him to do it."

Nat felt terrible, but not terrible enough to

confess. "Does your dad paint fairies and dragons too?" she asked.

"No," said Penny, "he mostly paints houses. Oh, and he's doing the bus stops in the town centre this week."

Everything was still going well for Nat as the open evening began. *Dad's finally done something right,* Nat thought, as yet another visitor said how good her picture was, and how they especially liked her pet pig.

"This is Mr and Mrs Thin-and-ugly," said the Head, introducing a very tall and stuck-up couple to Nat. She didn't actually say that, she said their proper names, but Nat was terrible with names. Dad had told her she should try to remember people by some memorable feature. So Mr and Mrs Thin-and-ugly it was, then.

"Mr Thin-and-ugly is Chairman of the Governors," said Mrs Trout, as if that meant something important.

"Hello," said Nat. "I'm Nathalia."

It turned out that Mr Thin-and-ugly considered himself to be very important, as he used to be in the army. Nat thought they might have used him for cleaning out the long barrels of the guns, but didn't say it. She'd tell Darius later. Where *was* Darius? She wondered if he had stayed for the open evening. She doubted it.

Heavens, the Head was still droning on.

"…budding artist… blossoming… a challenging parent… high hopes for her…"

No, the school would rather lock Darius in a cupboard than let him loose here tonight, Nat thought.

"Excellent idea," said Mr Thin-and-ugly. "Let us to the art room go." Some people speak like that. It's best to avoid them.

Bye, thought Nat, as they moved off. *Missing you already*. She looked out of the window. She thought she saw something moving from the corner of her eye.

"Well come on, dear," said Mrs Trout.

"What now?" said Nat, confused.

"Do pay attention. We're all going to the art room. Our star artist is going to draw a picture of them."

Nat stared back at her blankly.

"That's you, Nathalia."

"And can you draw us with a pig too?" said Mrs Thin-and-ugly.

Aaaaargh-nooooo, thought Nat. *I'm doomed.*

Ten minutes later and Nat was staring, in panic, at a piece of drawing paper on a large easel in the middle of the art room. A small crowd had gathered to watch the artist at work. She had insisted that no one look at the picture before she finished it. She'd put a sheet round the easel to hide the picture until it was done. She said that was what real artists did and she got a small round of applause. Mr and Mrs Thin-and-ugly (whom Nat was now calling Mr and Mrs I-hate-you-you've-ruined-my-life) were sitting stiffly in front of her.

Nat made another few strokes of her pencil

and accidentally added another nose. Or ear, it was hard to tell. *Oh rats*, she thought, *that's WORSE*. Which was hard to believe. Mr Thin-and-ugly looked like something wicked out of *Star Wars* and Mrs I-Hate-you etc. looked like something that had been left in the fridge for too long. Mr I-Hate-you etc. looked at his watch.

"You've moved – you've ruined it now," said Nat. "And I've decided I'm not in a drawing mood. Us artists are like that."

"Nonsense," said the Head firmly. "Don't be so temperamental. Unless you want to be in a 'picking up litter with Darius Bagley until you're in Year Thirteen' mood."

Nat swallowed hard.

"Please, please, give the artist *room*... She can't be expected to CREATE in a pressured environment like this," said Miss Glossop, the drippy art teacher.

Nat nodded her thanks, then after a few moments, she threw a sheet over the easel.

"Done," she said, still playing for time. "You

can all go now, thank you. Bye." There was more applause. "Well, unveil it, child," said Mrs Troutfish.

"What, now?" said Nat.

"Oh, give it here." The Head grabbed at the easel. Nat grabbed at the easel. "Just a few more minutes," she pleaded desperately. "It's not quite ready. The – ah – the paint hasn't dried."

But it was to no avail. Mrs Trout raised her eyebrows and Nat's fingers loosened their grip. Dad had really dropped her in it this time. She was done for.

"Coming through," shouted Darius, out of nowhere, "Beep beep." He was hurtling down the corridor towards the open art-room door, little legs a blur, carrying a large sack of rubbish in one hand and a pointy stick in the other. "Out of my way – litter police."

"Ow," said several people who were jabbed with the pointy stick.

"Must make it tidy," shouted Darius, picking up speed and waving the stick. "Important people here."

The running-twitching-poking-shouting boy bashed into the visitors like a rocket-powered dodgem car. He knocked people left, right and centre as he hurtled straight into the crowd. The Head made a grab for him but he was too small and quick. Besides, she wasn't absolutely sure she wanted to touch him without wearing rubber gloves.

"Crisp-packet patrol," shouted Darius. "Urgent. Nee-naw nee-naw."

"Watch where you're going, you revolting child,"

shouted the Chair of the Governors, just managing to avoid the pointy stick.

"Ronald, do something," said his wife, diving out of the way, but NOT avoiding the pointy stick. "Ow! It's gone mad."

"What do you suggest?" asked the Chair, using his wife as a human shield. "I'm not allowed to shoot people any more."

Darius reached Nat and started running round in circles, near the easel. He nudged it and it tipped up, balanced on one leg. "Watch out, the picture's going over! Catch it!" said the Chair, who was standing far enough away that he wouldn't risk having to catch it himself, so felt safe to say "Catch it!" to other people. He had learned this trick in the army.

Too late. With a crash the easel fell to the ground. Darius somehow got himself tangled up in the sheet, and began thrashing about, like a captured sea creature.

"Don't you dare kick him," shouted Nat, noticing the Chair taking a crafty run-up.

"Must – pick – up – all – litter," said Darius in his best robot voice, over the sound of ripping noises. Finally several of the braver prospective parents hauled the boy out of the mess and picked him up, wriggling. Most had now decided they didn't want their children to come to *this* school, thank you.

Nat's picture was in little tiny pieces on the end of his stick. Darius had saved her! He winked at her and she played along: "Oh no," she said, "that horrible boy has ruined my lovely painting. I'm so upset and things."

Tee hee, she thought, *well done, chimpy, the cheese and onion crisps are on me tomorrow.*

But as he was carted off to the Head's office, she suddenly wondered what was going to happen to him. By the look on Mrs Trout's face, it wasn't going to be good.

CHAPTER FIFTEEN

• • • •

Darius wasn't in Nat's class the next day. She didn't need to ask where he was; it was horribly obvious. Halfway through her first lesson she said she was feeling sick and could she get some water. She went past the room with the naughty, scary kids and sure enough, there he was, sitting on his own. He was the smallest there. He was talking to himself. Two of the older kids were fighting and his desk was knocked over before the teacher broke it up, coloured pencils scattering on the floor. Darius looked at

Nat through the glass in the door but she hurried past.

It was all her fault. She felt terrible. Then she remembered it was actually Dad's fault and felt a bit better.

And while it was nice that she could hang out with Penny and Abi and Frankeee and the other, normal girls, who were at last very almost talking to her, she had to admit – it wasn't nearly as much fun without Darius. There was no one to make silly jokes in English, no one to make eyeball farts in history, no one to jump out of a cupboard in geography and no one to help her with what the heck 'x' was in maths.

Maybe that was why Dad did it. Maybe he saw she was a bit glum and was trying to do something to cheer her up, in a Dad way. That was the nicest reason Nat could think of, for what Dad did next.

Nat was eating her breakfast the next day, listening to Kerri, Bonehead and Cabbage rabbit on, as usual. Dad had disappeared off somewhere while Nat was shovelling down her second bowl of cereal. The DJs were having a phone-in on the topic, 'The most embarrassing thing I ever did.'

"We've got our old mate Ivor on the line," Nat heard Cabbage say. "That's just brilliant."

Nat could tell he didn't mean it. *This sounds fun*, she thought. *And what a coincidence too – my dad's called Ivor. Oh no, hang on...*

"YEAH, and apparently he's got embarrassing stories about US," said Kerri nervously. "Wonder what they can be?" said Bonehead, who sounded like he didn't want to know.

Nat stopped eating, her spoon halfway to her mouth. She looked around and couldn't see Dad. Oh no, surely he wasn't... but he was. She heard Dad's voice – but not from the kitchen... from the RADIO.

Dad was live on air! Nat dropped her spoon in horror. This was going to be TERRIBLE. Dad was going to show her up AGAIN.

But then, as she listened, her fears subsided and she actually began to smile. Dad was properly very funny. Like Mum said he was, but he never seemed to be.

He told the listeners that Cabbage was scared of the dark, that Kerri was really called Lady Catherine Kensington-Rise, heir to the family's baked-bean fortune, and finally read out one of Bonehead's love poems to a girl called Jessica who would never go out with him at college because he was ginger.

Nat laughed so hard at the lines...

When I see you, my lips do tingle/it's valentine's day and I'm still single. All the king's horses and all the king's men/couldn't put my heart together again/not without proper medical training and an ambulance.

...that milk shot out of her nose.

There was a lot of fake laughing as the DJ's pretended to find this funny. Then things turned a bit nasty. "I seem to remember something embarrassing about you, though," said Bonehead.

Nat's blood froze. "Hang up, Dad," she shouted.

Dad didn't hang up. "What's that, then?" he asked good-naturedly.

"Hang up, Dad," shouted Nat more loudly, leaving the kitchen and looking for him.

"Your name's pretty embarrassing, isn't it?" said Kerri.

"HANG UP, DAD!" shouted Nat, up the stairs.

"Oh, I don't think so," said Dad. "Everyone knows it's pronounced *Bew-mole-ay*. No one laughs at that."

"AAAARRRGH, HANG UP, DAD!" shouted Nat, crashing into his bedroom, where he was chatting on the phone. "In fact, my daughter Nathalia tells me no one at her new school has even noticed yet. I mean, it does look a bit funny written down; it's spelled—"

"Nooooo," shouted Nat, leaping for the phone.

"B – U – M – O – L – E."

"BUM HOLE, BUM HOLE," shouted the DJs gleefully.

Nat grabbed the receiver off him and slammed it down. "Dad," she yelled, "everyone at school listens to that. What have you done???"

She found out soon enough. As she walked into class that day, there was a teeny microsecond pause which gave her the even teensier hope that no one had heard the— Oh wait, no...

"BUM HOLE, BUM HOLE, BUM HOLE, BUM HOLE," rang out round the room, as the whole class laughed and pointed and chanted her awful name.

Some of the more musical children sang harmonies and four had started a barber-shop quartet especially.

She knew it was bound to happen sooner or later, but that didn't make it better. Anyone who can't imagine what that day was like simply hasn't been to school. It seemed like EVERYONE had heard the radio show. Which was soon available as a podcast. The only reason the school-wide teasing wasn't worse was because Nat was friends with Darius Bagley. Kids thought he was just weird enough to be dangerous. And yet with Darius in the naughty class, there was no one actually around to make it better. She was finished.

"Everyone's teasing me except Penny Posnitch, and I'm not sure she counts because half the time she thinks she lives in Narnia with the tree fairies and now I've got no friends and it's all your fault," she wailed at Dad when she got home later that day. Fortunately, Mum was home early that night and immediately made things much better. Mainly by shouting at Dad a lot.

"What did you think you were playing at?" Nat heard her say. "I told you years ago we should have given Nathalia my name but you refused to see the problem. You just think everything is funny and you know what, life's not like that, Ivor. I wish it was."

"It all depends on how you look at things," said Dad quietly.

Mum suddenly stopped shouting at Dad. Her temper was like Nat's – up and down in a flash. She kissed Dad. *Urgh*, thought Nat, *old people kissing*. "I love the way you look at things," Mum said gently, "and I just wish the rest of the world was as lovely and daft as you are but it's not."

Dad sighed. Nat very nearly felt sorry for him.

"I'm taking Nat out for late-night shopping and pizza," said Mum, "and you can stay here and think about how to make things better."

Mum bought Nat some new shoes and a new pencil case, even though she didn't need them. Then she sat her down over a big cheesy pizza and told her that life was pretty tough on everyone, although the normal rules didn't seem to apply to Dad. Mum always made Nat feel grown up. *If only Mum could do the same with Dad*, Nat thought as they made their way home.

But, amazingly, when they got back, Dad had actually had a REALLY GOOD IDEA.

"We'll have a party," said Dad, as they walked

through the door.

"What sort of a party?" asked Mum.

"A birthday party. For Nat."

"Excellent idea. But her birthday's not till next year," said Mum. "And you were supposed to be thinking of ways to make things better NOW."

"I KNOW her birthday's next year," said Dad. "But they don't, do they? We'll invite all the class, throw a brilliant party and you'll make lots of friends, won't you, Nat! They'll soon forget about the silly name thing after that."

There was a pause. "It's not a bad idea," admitted Nat. "But can Mum organise it?"

She noticed Dad looked hurt. Then she saw that Mum had seen it too.

"Oh, come on, Nat, let Dad do it. He wants to make it up to you. Besides, he doesn't get *everything* wrong."

There was another pause.

"Well exactly," said Dad, when he realised Nat wasn't going to agree. "AND it gives me a chance to show the parents that I can organise something that's not a total disaster."

"Only if the party's not a total disaster," said Mum sternly. "So don't go overboard. Make sure you keep it simple."

"Oh, come on," said Dad. "It's a kids' party. Jellies, ice cream, pin the tail on the donkey – how hard can it be? I mean, what sort of parties do kids expect these days?"

CHAPTER SIXTEEN

• • • •

IT TURNED OUT THEY EXPECTED QUITE A LOT.

"What sort of party, Bumhole?" asked classmate after classmate.

"A birthday party," replied Nat again and again.

"Yes, but what sort of Bumhole birthday party?" they all answered back. "What's the theme? What's the entertainment? What's the unique selling point?"

"It's a surprise," replied Nat truthfully, thirty times.

But the mysterious approach wasn't working. Her classmates needed details. Then Nat had another genius idea. Mum always said that in business you had to find out what people wanted, then give it to them. So that's what she would do.

She started with Penny. "You'll like my party," she said. "It's the sort... you'll really like."

"What, has it got fairy face painting? Oh, I love fairy face painting."

"Oh yeah," said Nat. "There's lots of fairy face painting." *Ha ha ha, this is easy*, thought Nat, moving on to another classmate. *See you on Saturday, sucker.*

Now, it's fair to say what happened next was not what Dad had in mind for the party. He thought Nat was going to find out what sort of party *most* kids would like. Nat's idea was to make sure she threw a party that *everyone* would like.

"So what sort of party is it to be, love?" said Dad when she got home that night.

"Hang on," said Nat, "I'll consult my

notebook." She reached into her schoolbag, which she'd dumped on the sofa. Dad looked puzzled and a bit worried as she rummaged around for her book.

"OK, here we go. Eight kids want a football party. Skating, five votes, seven if we include ice-skating. Bowling, ten. Seven want zombie shooting with real zombies. Go-karts, fourteen – which was a surprise; I thought that would be more popular. Bouncy castle, always a safe bet, twenty votes, street-dance demonstration ten votes, magicians six, although we have to keep them away from Lauren O'Reilly who's got a phobia. Cookery demonstrations are *very* popular this year, specially if someone from the telly's coming to make cupcakes."

She paused, but only for breath. "Then there's the usual – face painting, jugglers and a best-kept pet competition. And everyone still expects party bags and balloon animals, except Flora Marling who's allergic to rubber."

She paused happily. "I think that covers it."

"So? Which one do you want to do?" said Dad nervously.

"ALL of them Dad, obviously. Don't you get it? I said yes to everything. And now everyone's coming. This Saturday's gonna be the best day of my life."

Dad put down his fork. For once he seemed to be lost for words.

Nat had a wonderful week. She felt like Queen Bee instead of Princess Bumhole. It seemed everyone was excited about the amazing party on Saturday. Her whole class was talking about it.

The only cloud on her horizon was Darius, still stuck with the horrible kids. She felt really guilty; it was her fault he was in there, and yet she was making more friends without him. Maybe it was because Mum was right and Dad was wrong – life was really tough and not that funny at all.

Then on Friday lunchtime, the most incredible thing happened. She had avoided the lunch crowd she'd been surrounded by for the last few days and gone looking for Darius. They had hardly spoken since he was moved to the horrible class and she wasn't sure what to say to him. "Thanks," didn't seem like enough. *But*, she told herself, *it was better than nothing*. She found him in the dining room sitting on his own, talking to himself. He looked a bit lost. She was just walking over to him, when suddenly Flora Marling appeared in front of her and simply said, "Hi."

"Hi," squeaked Nat. Flora was the one person who hadn't yet said she was coming to the 'birthday' party. And now she was standing right in front of her, flanked by the three girls who followed her everywhere. No one cared what they were called; in everyone's eyes they were just Flora's minions.

Nat couldn't take her eyes off Flora's hair. It was as perfect and golden and shiny and bouncy as her older sister's – and *she* was in a shampoo advert. Nat realised her hand had begun to stretch out to touch it…

"See you tomorrow, I guess," said Flora with a hint of a smile. Nat snatched her hand away in shock. This was a-mazing! Flora Marling nodded her perfect head sharply towards Darius, who was eating peas off his knife. "Is IT coming?"

And then Nat did something terrible. "What? No!" Nat heard herself say. It was as if something had taken over her body. She couldn't help it, and even worse she added the words, "We're not like *friends* or anything."

Flora laughed and the three minions laughed too. Nat laughed as well, far too loudly, and then, as quickly as she'd appeared, Flora Marling was gone. Nat stood still for a few moments in triumph. Then just as quickly, she felt sick. She desperately hoped Darius hadn't heard her.

But when she looked over to where he had been sitting, he was gone. Nat realised she'd got a nasty taste in her mouth, and just for once it wasn't from the school dinners.

She avoided Darius at break, because she felt so rotten. Rotten mixed with happy, because no one made a bum joke, and FLORA MARLING WAS COMING TO HER PARTY!!!

Every time she thought about going to talk to Darius, someone else would come and say hello and that they were looking forward to Saturday. Inside Nat, her little Nat-shaped Evil Villain tried to tell her she'd done the right thing and that the path to popularity was a harsh one, but even she could tell this little Evil Villain's heart wasn't in it.

The next time she saw Darius, he was standing with Miss Hunny by the school gates at home time. She was going to have to walk past him. She just KNEW he'd heard her, and even if by some miracle he hadn't, he would have realised by now that he wasn't invited to her party. She couldn't move; she couldn't face him. Then she heard,

"Cooee! Only me. Over here. Your dad couldn't pick you up because he's hurt his back helping lay the Astroturf. It'll probably be a discombobulated disc, I shouldn't wonder. He'll never tango again, poor man."

It was Bad News Nan at the gates. *Saved again!* thought Nat. Although Bad News Nan's driving was as frightening as her stories (both were full of pain and suffering and pretty sure to end terribly). The moment Bad News Nan saw Darius she grabbed him and gave him a big hug. His head got stuck in her bosom and Nat watched as his little legs wriggled while he suffocated. Nat seized her chance to dash past while Darius couldn't see her for bosom. "Meet you at the car, Nan," shouted Nat, running past.

"That's your friend from the other night, isn't it?" said Nan as she pulled away without looking. Nathalia stared out of the window. "I hadn't realised he was a Bagley. Poor little thing."

"What do you mean?" said Nat nervously. She had a horrible feeling about this, just as she had a horrible feeling about Nan's terrible driving.

Nan was always like that. She could never remember anyone's name until she discovered something tragic about them. Nan never forgot a name after that.

Bad News Nan told Nat that Darius had no parents. Nat missed why – she had put her head in the crash position during a near-miss with a lorry. But they might have been in prison or on the run or been pecked to death by emus at a safari park, it didn't really matter. Darius had already moved house about ten times, being shoved between various Bagley clan members until they got fed up with him. He was now living with his older brother...

Oswald Bagley.

Ban News Nan said that name as if expecting horror music to suddenly blare out. "What's wrong with Oswald Bagley?" asked Nat. There was a silence. Bad News Nan was gripping the steering wheel and looking straight ahead. "I don't know anything about him," she said finally.

Oh no, thought Nat.

Grown-ups fool themselves that kids don't know when they're fibbing. News flash for parents, THEY DO KNOW, IDIOTS. Nat knew Bad News Nan was fibbing. And if Bad News Nan didn't want to talk about him, he must be very bad indeed.

She knew this, just as she knew that Darius, her little farty gibbering twitching burping BETRAYED friend Darius, needed her. The friend who made her laugh, let her cheat at maths, always stuck up for her, and saved her from the art-room disaster. THAT friend. And she'd let him down.

Bad News Nan hadn't finished talking. "Still, at least he has you as a friend, eh?" she said.

CHAPTER SEVENTEEN

• • • •

"DAD, GET UP OFF THE SOFA! WE'VE GOT TO GO round to Darius's house NOW. I've made a terrible mistake," shouted Nat breathlessly as she bounded into her house. Exactly two seconds later she was sprawled face first on the hall lino.

"Careful of the generator cables," shouted Dad, exactly two seconds too late. Nat got up, then dragged Dad off the sofa, Bad News Nan's words ringing in her ears.

Five minutes later they were in the Atomic

Dustbin, heading to the Paradise Estate. Nat thought whoever named it had a weirder sense of humour than Dad. The road they were now on was lined on either side with run-down houses and mean-looking, low-rise flats. There were bunches of huddled shops with their front metal grilles pulled down so you couldn't tell what they sold. As they drove past, Nat saw a hand-written sign. 'Eight cans for a pound,' it read.

Right at the very edge of the estate sat a small, scruffy house with an even scruffier garden, full of rubbish. It had dirty white pebbledash walls with grimy plastic-framed windows. Brown tiles hung crookedly on the roof, like teeth in a tramp's mouth. There was a goat in the garden, munching weeds. Outside was a large black motorbike. Oswald Bagley's motorbike.

Dad parked the van and turned the engine off. It became clear that something inside the house was howling. "That's never a good sign," said Dad. The Dog shot under the table, paws over his ears, trembling.

"I don't think Darius's brother likes visitors," said Nat. "Darius told me that someone came to read the electricity meter once and was never seen again."

Dad tutted. "That's silly," he said.

"No, it's true," insisted Nat, in the voice she used for telling ghost stories. "Postmen refuse to even walk up the path. Look…" She pointed to a pile of letters in brown envelopes stuffed under a brick in the garden.

"Darius is your friend," said Dad. Nat had told him what she had done to Darius on the way here. "Saying sorry and inviting him to the party is the right thing to do." Dad sounded quite fierce. He opened the van door and hopped out. Ten seconds later he hopped back in again. "That is VERY loud howling," he said. The Dog was shivering with fear.

"Can't we just phone him?" said Nat, now a bit nervous. Dad thought for a moment. "No, Miss Hunny said their phone's been cut off."

Nat grabbed Dad. "Look…" she said pointing

to a patch of freshly dug earth in the front garden. "The phone man is probably buried next to the electricity man."

"Maybe Oswald likes gardening," said Dad unconvincingly. "On the radio they said it's a good time to plant rhubarb."

"That's not rhubarb," whispered Nat, "it's a shallow grave."

Finally they got out of the van (the cowardly Dog did not) and walked slowly up the path to the house. There were half a dozen locks on the door. "Not sure who'd want to break in," said Dad.

"No, the locks are there to stop anyone getting *out...*" said Nat.

Dad took a deep breath and prepared to knock. "At least the howling's stopped," he said. Suddenly something threw itself against the front door with a massive wallop, and the howling started again.

"Aaargh!" shouted Nat, running back down the path.

And straight into Oswald Bagley.

Ten minutes later, Nat, Oswald, Darius and Dad were sitting awkwardly in the Bagleys' front room, in silence. The room was small and cluttered and smelt of cabbage and chip fat. There were no family photos or any other pictures on the walls, just a huge TV in the corner. The sound was turned down but Oswald's eyes were still glued to it. Something hairy that was either a huge dog or a small bear was lying at Dad's feet, snarling. Every so often it looked at Oswald as if to say, "Can I eat him *now*?"

Oswald drank something out of a can. He hadn't offered one to Dad, or a cup of tea or anything. Nat noticed that Dad didn't seem to quite know what to do with his hands, apart from keep them out of the way of doggie teeth.

"He won't hurt you while Oswald's here," said Darius unconvincingly.

Dad leaned towards Darius. "Nathalia's got something to say."

The two children looked at each other. Dad had a look on his face that said, *I'm very proud of my little girl. This is a moment I will treasure forever.*

"Soz, farty," said Nat.

"S'all right, Buttface," said Darius.

And that was the treasured moment.

"While I'm here…" began Dad. Nat looked at him. Surely it was just time to escape now? Two words kept circling round her head – shallow… grave… shallow… grave…

But Dad burbled on. "You must be worried about Darius getting moved to that special class," he said.

Oswald just shrugged and carried on watching. People on the TV were arguing angrily with each other, silently shouting. A fight had started and Darius's brother laughed. Dad fidgeted uncomfortably.

"Anything you can think of to help…" said Dad, voice trailing off. Oswald just carried on staring at the TV.

Dad elbowed Nat. He clearly wanted her to say something. Nat looked around. She tried to think of something nice to say about Darius's house. She knew that's what normal people did when they went to normal people's houses. After a few minutes all she could think of was,

"That's a nice fish tank. Do you think the smelly upside-down floaty fish are OK?"

Or,

"I like the way my chair is made from beer crates and copper wire and it only needs a cushion to stop me being in *incredible bum pain.*"

Or,

"Most people repair broken windows with expensive glass. How economical to use a bin liner."

So she didn't say anything. Neither did Darius. Nat wasn't sure Oswald *could* speak, and even Dad gave up talking in the end. He nodded to Nat and they stood up to leave.

"See you tomorrow to spoil my party, then?" said Nat.

"Yeah," said Darius. "It'll be rubbish though."

As Oswald closed the door, Nat saw Darius's pale face through the window giving her a weak smile. Nat reached for Dad's hand as they walked back to the van.

CHAPTER EIGHTEEN

• • • •

Nat's party began at 5am. Or rather, it began for Dad at 5am. She was fast asleep and was not even a little bit disturbed by Dad stumbling sleepily about the kitchen, walking into things and looking for teabags.

Mum had got back late the night before and had left a note by the kettle. It said,

'I've worked eighty hours this week. Wake me early and DIE.'

The last word was written in red ink and underlined six times.

Nat, however, had specifically asked to be woken. Last night she'd said,

"Dad, there's so much to do tomorrow you HAVE to wake me up REALLY early, OK?"

But now when Dad tried to rouse her she said, "What are you doing? Get lost. It's so early it's still yesterday. If I get up now I'll have panda eyes for my party – is that what you want? Go AWAY." And burrowed back under the covers.

Half dozing, Nat imagined what Dad was doing. She reckoned he'd start by drinking two cups of tea and making a 'To do' list.

When Nat came downstairs a few hours later and found Dad's list, she smugly congratulated herself on guessing right.

The list went like this:

Make tea.

06:00 – Make 100 sandwiches: Cheese. ham. chocolate spread. fish paste. crisps.

07:00 – Open 15 packets of mini sausages. 15 packets of mini Scotch eggs. 15 packets of mini pizzas.

07:10 – Open one packet of salad leaves. just in case.

07:15 – Organise roller rink, go-karts, bouncy castle, trampoline, magician, clown, dancers, cookery demonstration, face painters, invent some party games and tidy house.

08:00 – Shower, change.

08:30 – Finish off those cracker jokes that were due last week.

11:30 – Chillax, ready to meet very impressed parents.

Then she saw Dad asleep at the kitchen table and felt a bit less smug. He had only made six sandwiches.

When she woke him up he admitted that he had run out of bread, butter, cheese, ham, chocolate spread, fish paste and crisps. And he'd forgotten to buy the mini sausages, mini Scotch eggs and mini pizzas. So he couldn't get much further until the shops opened. He asked if he could give the kids what he had left in the freezer.

"No, Dad," wailed Nat. "Pork chops, battered cod and garden peas ARE NOT party food. DON'T SHOW ME UP. I told you, the average age of people at my party is 11.265547 years – Darius worked it out. So you have to do food that someone who is 11.265547 years old will like."

I can't be more accurate than that, can I? she thought, annoyed. *I've done it to six decimals.*

By 9:00, the chaos had really begun. The workmen delivering the mini roller-skating rink were already arguing with the workmen who were trying to construct the kiddy go-kart track. They were shouting and marching in and out of the garden, wiping their muddy boots on the lino.

"There wasn't enough room for all of us," said Steve, the workman in charge of the rink to a pale-looking Dad. "So we've moved your garden shed and Dave and Barry are busy taking down your greenhouse."

Something that sounded horribly like panes of glass smashing could be clearly heard over noisy machinery and even noisier radios.

"We were here first," said Kevin, the man in charge of the go-kart team. He was yelling over the sound of a generator and the current number one hit single. "Tell this lot to take their silly roller-rink back. It's no good for a kids' party anyway."

"You're just jealous cos we're getting more business than you these days," said Roller-rink Steve, and turned up his radio.

"Only because they've got skating all over the telly at the moment. Flash in the pan, mate," said Go-kart Kevin, turning up HIS radio.

"And another thing," Roller-rink Steve continued. "Turn your horrible radio off. No one wants to listen to the news at this time in the morning. We all like to hear music when we're working."

"Yeah, well your *average* workman does," replied Go-kart Kevin. "But we're a bit smarter than the average. More educated. I've got twelve GCSEs out working in this garden."

"You saying we're thick?" said Roller-rink Steve, taking a step towards him. "What's the capital of Venezuela? Answer me that, clever clogs."

Before the situation got any uglier, the men coming to inflate the bouncy castle turned up, and they told Dad that there was no way he could have the mini roller rink, kiddy go-kart track and Baron Boingy's Super Castle of Springy Fun in the same garden.

"Not my fault, mate, it's 'ealth and safety. Blame Europe," said the bouncy castle operator, a mister Bernie Spratt. Dad gave Mr Spratt some money to make the European problem go away. "Now there's a lesson in politics for you," he said to Nat with a smile.

"WHAT THE HELL IS ALL THIS NOISE?" shouted Mum, appearing in her dressing gown.

As if by magic, all the noise stopped.

"Now, boys," she said, in a sweet voice that was somehow way more frightening than her shouty voice, "there's a café round the corner – go and get your breakfasts. Be back in half an hour. Not you, Ivor," she added to Dad, who was trying to slope off with the workmen. "I want a word with you."

The men trooped out quietly. One or two of them muttered "Sorry, mate," and "Wouldn't fancy being in your shoes," to Dad as they went past.

"Cup of tea, love?" said Dad nervously, to break the uncomfortable silence that was filling the kitchen. Mum sat down, and then in her most quiet and considered voice that she only brought out on very special occasions and was even more scary than all her other scary voices, said, "Yes, please, darling. And then you can tell me exactly what you've been up to this week."

Nat knew what was coming and slid out of the kitchen. She listened from the safe side of the door, though.

"Where the heck did you find the money for all this?" Mum exploded, as Dad listed the events. "Have you sold the world's most expensive joke? Or is THIS the world's most expensive joke?"

"That's very good," said Dad, who could appreciate a good joke. *Nooooo*, thought Nat,

Mum isn't REALLY joking.

"You know I've been at a conference all week," shouted Mum, "away from home trying to earn enough money to keep you in pork pies and a roof over my little girl's head. Do you mean to say that as soon as my back was turned you decided to waste it all?"

"You wanted me to organise it," said Dad, which was true.

"I SAID keep it simple," said Mum, which was also true. "How much have you actually spent?"

Nat put her fingers in her ears. She wasn't THAT nosy. But it must have been loads because Mum was now making a noise like a steam kettle chucked into a volcano.

"WHAT?" she yelled. "HOW MUCH? Don't you dare tell me you've spent all our holiday money on a bouncy castle."

"Not just a bouncy castle. There's a mini roller rink and a kiddy go-kart and a—"

Nat heard a noise like something smashing. *A*

teapot, perhaps, she thought.

"That money was so we could go somewhere hot."

"I thought we might stay at home this year."

"You ARE staying at home. Me and Nathalia are going somewhere hot." Then after a moment, she continued, "Do you think this is not now going to end up as a COMPLETE disaster like everything else you get your hands on? And who is it that has to be Mrs Sensible and clear up your mess? Oh, I despair."

Ten minutes later Mum was getting into her little red car. She was booked in to get her hair done for the party. "I'm sorry, Nat," she said. "I'll be longer than I thought. I might have to go for a massage too. I do love your father but if I don't get relaxed RIGHT NOW I'm going to strangle him with a balloon animal." And with that she drove off at speed.

Just you and me then, Dad, thought Nat, feeling ever-so-slightly sick.

"Right," said Dad, doing a rubbish impression of a really confident person as he hopped into the Atomic Dustbin, "I have to go to the cash and carry to buy the rest of the party food. Plus some balloons, plates, streamers, squash and a new teapot. If the neighbours come round to complain about the noise and the mess and the damage, don't forget to cough."

"Cough?" said Nat suspiciously.

"Yeah, I told them the party was only this massive because it was a charity fundraiser. Your medical treatment's really expensive. Bye."

What followed was one of the most uncomfortable hours of Nat's life, sitting silently with their two furious neighbours.

"Dad won't be long," she kept saying. She coughed again. "It's not catching," she added feebly.

Mr Pringle from Number 17 made a snorting noise and folded his arms tightly across his belly. He tutted through his bushy top lip and his lumpy nose sniffed in disapproval at the very idea.

Mr Pringle disapproved of everything Nathalia had to offer – from toast to biscuits to coffee to a mini super fun park currently being put up in the garden. Mr Dinkins from number 13 shook his head apologetically. His thin lips were wet, their smile was forced. "Very kind, but my stomach is too delicate this morning. Something has upset my system. I cannot for the life of me imagine what it was. Unless it was being woken by a gang of hooligans driving a large van into my front garden and squashing my begonias."

Nat laughed nervously. "Fancy a free go on the bouncy castle?" she tried lamely. Then to her relief she heard the roar of a large motorbike pulling up outside.

"Front door's open," said Darius, walking in a minute later. "I've come to help out. Got any Hobnobs?" The Dog leapt up and licked his face. Darius wiped the slobber off and with THE SAME HAND rummaged about in the biscuit barrel.

After five minutes of Darius's company,

during which time he entertained the neighbours with eyeball farts, headstands, the joke about the constipated owl and three new verses of the diarrhoea poem, both neighbours left, muttering darkly that they hoped she got well soon but they wanted to see Dad the second he returned.

Nat looked at Darius. He'd saved her AGAIN! But before she could say anything…

"Cooee. Only me. I'd have got here sooner but my car died. And then on the bus the woman next to me had a fainting fit and we had to wrap her in a silver blanket. I offered to go with her to the hospital but she said I was making her feel worse. Must have been delirious."

What was Bad News Nan doing at her party?? thought Nat.

"Ooh, is there any birthday cake?" said Bad News Nan, bustling into the kitchen. "If I just dig out a slice from the bottom no one will notice."

A second later, Dad rushed into the house with ten bags of terrible toxic frozen food and a gallon of orange-type, glow-in-the-dark squash.

Seeing Bad News Nan, and Nat's face, Dad said sheepishly, "Sorry, I thought she could help."

They watched as Bad News Nan attacked the cake. "Not too much cos it gets under me plate," she said, shovelling down a brick-sized cakey wedge.

"That little boy on the roof reminds me of Edna's grandson."

"Edna…?" said Dad weakly.

"Edna Pottingshed. Lived next door to us when you were three. Moved away when her grandson fell off the roof on to Mr Anderson's chickens. Didn't survive."

Nat didn't wait to find out who didn't survive – the chickens or Edna Pottingshed's grandson. She went to call Darius down from the roof.

She was now getting that horrible sinking feeling she got whenever Dad planned anything.

Not today, she pleaded to the god of little girls with embarrassing dads. *Please let it be OK today…*

Fortunately, once Nat had got Darius down from the roof, the workmen distracted her from her misery by getting her to help out. She and Darius spent an hour holding and pulling and fetching and carrying, and then another hour welcoming the entertainers. These included Ali Kadabra the magician, Tippi Sparkle the face painter, and Martha Fudge the famous cake maker from off the telly. Nat was very excited to meet Mrs Fudge until Dad told her she was only a lookalike from an agency.

"The real Mrs Fudge wanted fifteen grand and a stretch limo just to turn up and put the frosting on a cupcake," explained Dad, as people started arriving. "This is just as good. Admittedly we've got a slight problem – she can't cook. At least, I think that's what she says – she's got a very strong Polish accent. That might count as two problems. Anyway, I've already hired an outdoor kitchen for her demo. I think I'll slip her a few quid to have a go at making cakes, but don't be surprised if they don't taste very nice."

Nat looked around. It was happening. Her party. Against all odds – i.e. Dad organising it – her party was actually looking pretty amazing. She ran excitedly upstairs to put her party clothes on. Maybe, JUST MAYBE, Dad might have pulled it off.

CHAPTER NINETEEN

••••

B Y THE TIME NAT CAME BACK DOWN, HER GUESTS WERE beginning to arrive. Nat was surprised but pleased to see everyone had brought presents. She hadn't even thought of that. Result! Darius caught her looking greedily at the parcels piling up in the front room.

"I never said it was my actual, proper BIRTHDAY," she said carefully, "just that it was my birthday PARTY."

Darius, who knew perfectly well it wasn't her birthday, shrugged and tore open a parcel.

"Hey!" said Nat as he wandered off with a nice Lego kit. "Happy birthday, Buttface," he said, grinning.

Nat was really beginning to enjoy herself now, swanning around, showing off to all her classmates.

"Your dad is amazing," said Penny Posnitch, who had bought Nat a poster of a unicorn. "I don't know why you moan about him all the time."

By now Nat was getting used to the idea that OK, fair enough, just MAYBE this wasn't going to be a Dad disaster after all. She was thrilled to see most of the children from her class looking impressed at everything on offer. Baron Boingy's bouncy castle was inflated, the go-karts were revved, the roller rink gleamed in the spring sunshine and most of the entertainers were set up and ready to entertain. *Yeah, Dad's actually pulled it off for once*, she thought.

Even Dad was walking around beaming.

"This is a great party. I can't think why none of

the parents want to stay," Dad said to Nat as yet another mum and dad disappeared faster than a magician's assistant. "Every time I ask they look at me as if I've offered them dog food."

Doh, thought Nat. *They've all got an afternoon off, haven't they?*

Parent after parent arrived and left. And they didn't just bring the invited child, they brought all their other kids too. "Hope there's room for a little one," they said, shooing their entire overexcited brood through the door before Dad could object.

Stanley Fletcher's parents were by far the worst. They arrived massively late, shoved their little boy through the front door, told Dad he had a terrible and dangerous nut allergy, handed him a MASSIVE NEEDLE filled with anti-allergy medicine and then ran out for an afternoon of Stanley-free fun. "If he eats a nut by accident and turns blue, just shove the needle in his rear end and give it a good squeeze," said Stanley's dad, backing away down the drive. "So kind, so generous. Hope to see you at a committee meeting soon, bye."

The committee was the only dampener to Nat's joy in this moment. If the party went well, the committee might decide to give Dad another chance after all. And no one could deny it – it WAS going well. However, Nat was prepared to make sacrifices to get popular. Besides, she figured, Dad was bound to do something stupid one day. Hopefully before the end of term disco.

Which he actually did a moment later, when he said,

"Darius, come down from Mr Pringle's extension, I need your help."

Darius jumped down on to a trampoline, bounced, and landed tidily at Dad's feet. The Dog came up and licked his sticky hand. "Clever boy," said Dad, to both of them, and both Darius and the Dog swelled with pride.

Dad looked Darius in the eye; most people didn't do that. "Darius, I'm putting you in charge. We seem to have collected a lot of little children. I need you to think of party games for them. I haven't got time to think of any so I'll leave that to you, OK?"

Dad then started off carrying a tray of dubious-looking hot party bites.

Just then, through the crowds of happy children, Nat noticed a halo of golden hair walking towards her.

"Dad, please don't show me up ANY MORE THAN USUAL in the next five minutes," she pleaded.

"Flora, Flora, over here," shouted Nat, waving to the beautiful golden-haired girl who had just arrived with two tall, good-looking parents.

Flora walked over to Nat and handed her a beautifully wrapped gift.

Behind The Golden One, Nat could see Darius come running, chasing a small crying boy. "I don't wanna play the flying game," wailed the little boy.

"Look!" said Nat to Flora, grabbing her shoulders and turning her anywhere away from

Darius. "Look at that."

"It's a fence," said Flora calmly.

"Um – yes, it is," said Nat lamely, "but it's a very nice one." Flora laughed. "You're funny," she said.

"Geronimo!" shouted Darius from somewhere. "AAAAAARGH!" shouted a little boy, from somewhere near Darius. Nat wasn't listening. She was in heaven. Flora Marling was at her party.

Flora Marling's parents were both doctors – her mother was a real one who wore a white coat and looked after patients; her father had become a doctor by writing books about people who write books. As Dad walked past with the tray of salty, sugary, fatty food full of artificial colourings, they both looked at him as if he was a failed science experiment, or a bad novel.

"Are you serving those for the children to eat?" asked Mrs Doctor Marling, slapping Flora's hand as she reached for one of the mini pizzas.

"Nothing I wouldn't eat myself," said Dad,

popping one in his mouth to demonstrate. It was still red hot. "Ah – ha – aaaaa," said Dad, as his tongue melted.

"We used to live round here," said Doctor Mister Marling. "Before we could afford to move."

"Ugh – ick – gah," said Dad, unable to spit the nuclear-hot morsel into the nearest bush, because he was aware of Nat's forbidding stare. "So – much – pain."

"Is your father ill?" said Doctor Mrs Marling. "I am a doctor." Like most doctors, she loved telling people she was a doctor.

"You've no idea," said Nat.

Dad finally swallowed the flaming piece of pizza. "You can't play football, can you?" he asked Mr Marling. "Only I've been let down at the last minute and I promised some of the boys there'd be someone from Manchester United coming. I probably aimed a bit high, I suppose. But you look a lot like their number four."

"I do not play football," said Mr Doctor

Marling, as if this was something to be proud of. Nat saw Flora roll her eyes up. Nat was getting that familiar clammy feeling... *Shut up Dad*, she screamed inside. *Shut up, shut UP.*

"Oh well," said Dad. "How do you feel about doing a turn as a clown? I've got the costume. I was going to do it myself but I haven't quite finished the sandwiches yet."

"Is anyone *responsible* in charge?" asked Mr Doctor Marling.

"Not really," admitted Nat.

And that was when Dad's final piece of entertainment arrived, and the unravelling of Nat's day could begin.

"Who are these creatures?" asked Mrs Doctor Marling, as a group of scantily-clad women high-stepped into the garden. They were all wearing sequins and short skirts and stockings and feathers. But they were not wearing many what you'd call 'proper clothes'.

"Oooh, get you, Mrs La-de-dah," said the woman with the most orange skin, most sequins and least clothing. "We're the dancers. I'm Trixie Forward." She held out her hand. Mrs Doctor Marling examined it as if she was looking for scabies.

"Of course you are," she said. "Flora, we're leaving. Right away."

"I think they're pretty," said Flora. "Can I wear that for my party?"

"No, you cannot," snapped Mr Doctor Marling.

"Dad..." wailed Nat. "Who are THEY? Do something."

Dad took Trixie to one side. "Why aren't you wearing more clothes?" he asked. "You don't look like street dancers. You should be in trainers and tracksuits. And why have you brought a pole?"

"You booked us," said Trixie, the leader of the group. "I printed out your booking form off the computer. Computer's don't lie." She pulled a form from her bra.

"Well, REALLY!" sniffed Mrs Doctor

Marling. "Outrageous."

"It's in black and white," Trixie explained reasonably. "It says here, 'Trixie Forward and her podium dance troupe'. I have the booking reference number too. It's all computerised these days. We're very modern."

"I thought podium was something to do with the Olympics," said Dad. "Something sporty."

"In THESE costumes?" said Trixie.

"I did it online, and I didn't have my glasses on," said Dad, flustered, as Nat kicked him in fury. "And it was really late and I was really tired."

"Well here's our booking reference number," said Trixie, not giving up.

"Well now he's un-booking you. Clear off," said Nat, desperately trying to get things back under control.

Trixie dug her high heels in. "You can't treat us like this. We've been given a job, and we're not leaving until we do it. Professional pride's at stake. Candii, put the music on. You're getting our act whether you like it or not."

"You are not dancing half naked in my garden in front of my little girl!" shouted Dad.

Nat cringed. "I'm not a little girl," she said, sounding like a little girl.

Dad was just as stubborn as Trixie Forward. "It's not suitable."

"Oh, go on, let them," shouted Roller-rink Steve, who was very glad he'd stayed behind to fix a roller skate.

"Yeah, let them, you big spoilsport," said Go-kart Kevin, who was very glad he'd stayed behind to fix a go-kart.

"You stay out of it," shouted Dad.

"No, she's right," said Mr Dinkins, leaning over the fence. "Professional pride – you heard her."

"This is a *children's* party," yelled Dad.

"We're not doing it for the children, we're doing it for you," said Trixie. "And for our dancing to be taken seriously. Candii, darling, music."

Candii turned on her portable CD player and the music started blaring out. The six girls took up their starting positions. By now a crowd of children was forming.

"I'm not staying here to be offended," shouted Mrs Doctor Marling.

"I suppose not," said Mr Doctor Marling. "Although we could stay, to see just how offended we are."

But his wife was already pushing him out of the garden. "Flora, come here now," she snapped, dragging her sighing daughter behind her.

And with that, Flora Marling was gone as if borne away by a sweet breeze, and Trixie Forward's Podium Dancers started their rather more spicy routine.

Dad rushed around the garden, rounding up children as quickly as he could. "Everyone inside the bouncy castle!" he shouted. "No, don't look round. It's a new game. Anyone turning round is out. Hurry, hurry."

From here, things went downhill. Fast. At

2pm, Dad got a call from Mum saying she had been caught a tiny bit speeding and would be a teeny bit late as she just might possibly have had a massive row with a policeman. She was now down the station helping them with their enquiries.

"I thought you were relaxed after your massage," Nat heard Dad say. Mum shouted at him so loudly that she thought his mobile was going to melt.

And to her horror Nat suddenly realised – her party was becoming yet another Dad Disaster.

CHAPTER TWENTY

••••

NAT LOOKED AROUND HER IN DESPAIR, AND EVERYWHERE she looked she saw utter mayhem.

Kids were bouncing each other on and off the castle, using the trampolines to launch themselves over the next-door neighbours' garden fences with happy yells. Mr Dinkins and Mr Pringle were missing, presumed hiding in their bedrooms.

Bigger and braver children were driving the little go-karts off the track in what could only be called an 'off-road adventure', destroying the garden and running over some of the smaller children, who couldn't get out of the way fast enough.

Long human chains were fast forming on the roller rink. This meant the adventurous child at the back of the line gained more speed than the average unmanned spacecraft. One or two ended up flying off and crashing into the hedge.

Nat noticed that Ali Kadabra seemed to be swigging from a bottle of something that looked suspiciously like gin, and was crying into his mobile phone.

Bad News Nan had stopped helping and was snoring on a deckchair, surrounded by heaps of crumbs. Someone had painted her face bright bottle green and Nat had a horrible feeling it was the paint from inside the shed that Dad used to paint the *outside* of the shed.

The cookery demonstration was going particularly badly because the kids didn't want a *lookalike* Mrs Fudge, they wanted a real one. A few of the more lively Year Sevens had started throwing bits of cake dough at her while she swore at them in Polish.

"Have you seen Darius and the little kids?"

Nat asked Dad nervously.

"They're the least of our worries," said Dad (wrongly, as it turned out). "They're all upstairs. He's doing something called the tangle game. You see I was right," said Dad, with a touch of pride. "Kids like Darius do ever so well if you give them a bit of responsibility. It makes them grow up."

You didn't, thought Nat, looking around at the madness.

"Oh dear, that's not Stanley Fletcher eating one of the Eastern European hazelnut cupcakes, is it?" said Dad nervously, as Stanley started to choke and turn blue.

Nat began to tear her hair out, as Dad dangled little Stanley Fletcher upside down, while trying to flick bits of cupcake out of his mouth.

"Is that all of it?" demanded Dad, shaking the poor boy rigorously. "Are you sure?" Stanley nodded, spitting bits of nutty cake on to Dad's shoes. Dad stood Stanley upright. "Shall I give you the needle now?"

"Aaargh!" screamed Stanley. "No needles!" and ran into the house. Dad chased after him, but only got as far as the patio when he tripped over the magician's box of tricks, just as Ali Kadabra was heading for the climax of his show. Two doves flew away into the sky, and a white rabbit hopped out, dashed across the grass and scuttled under the bouncy castle.

"Stop bouncing!" screamed Ali Kadabra to the kids on the castle. "You're squashing Mr Whiskers!" He grabbed Dad by the shoulders.

"I love that rabbit. He's all I've got now Karen's left me." Ali's lip trembled, his golden turban slipping over his eyes. "If anything happens to him I'm gonna make you disappear permanently." The magician suddenly hugged Dad tight. "She even took the dog," he sobbed. "Why did she take the *dog*?"

"It's all right," said Dad, patting him on the back kindly. "It's all right."

Ali pulled out a hanky to blow his nose. It was a string of hankies – white, yellow, pink, green.

The kids started laughing.

"It's not funny!" gasped the magician between sobs. "It's not part of the act." He sat down on the floor and cried. A car horn in his trousers went off, like a great fart. The kids howled with laughter.

"I'll kill you all!" screamed the crying conjurer and leapt off after them, tripping over his big shoes. More doves flew out of his hat as he waved it in rage. The children scattered, laughing as they ran.

Bad News Nan woke up as one kid careered into her deckchair. "Ooh, I had a terrible dream about the end of the world," she muttered, half asleep. She looked around the garden and saw that her dream had come true.

"Dad, this is a DISASTER!" shouted Nat furiously. "Everyone will say this is the worst party ever. DO SOMETHING!"

Dad looked around at the unravelling scene. Kids were clambering over the fences into the next-door neighbours' gardens. Someone had stolen all the face paints and decorated the fences with rude words and revolting pictures. Someone was crying in the kiddy go-kart track and it sounded like Mr Dinkins. Ali Kadabra was now weeping on Bad News Nan's crumb-covered bosom. "Never mind," she said, her face still bright green. "Tell me all about it. Especially the sad bits."

Year Seven swot Marcus Milligan, whose parents never let him eat sweets, had run amok. Buzzing on a half a dozen mini cheese substitute pizzas and three pints of orange-flavoured, glow-in-the-dark squash, he yelled, "Look at me, I can fly!" and chucked himself off Mr Pringle's extension, did a triple bounce off three trampolines and hurtled straight into next-door's leylandii tree, getting stuck six metres in the air.

As Dad ran to help, he noticed flames coming from lookalike Martha Fudge's outdoor kitchen. "I never said I could cook," she shouted. "I just look like her. I'm going home."

Nat ran to put the fire out. Penny Posnitch was already there, calmly throwing earth on the flames. Her face was sooty from the smoke. "You're needed upstairs," she said. "Something's gone wrong with Darius and the tangle game."

Nat took off like a rocket, not even realising

how relieved she was that at least one person was still talking to her.

Upstairs, the little kids were in a horrible, horrible mess. They were squashed up together in one big wriggling heap. This was the tangle game. The idea was to see how many kids could get into one big tangle. The only rule was that they had to hold hands at all times. Darius had helped them get properly tangled by using garden twine and superglue. He'd been hoping for a tangle game world record, but had got bored after a while and wandered off. There were now a dozen little children stuck fast and sobbing.

Nat started to untangle them when she looked out of the landing window and noticed one of her classmates walking off down the front drive with Mr Pringle's flat-screen telly. "What are you doing with that?" she shouted through the open window.

"I won it," said the boy. "Darius did bingo and I won. He said this was first prize."

"Well, it's not. And you can put that back

too," she yelled, as another boy walked past with a toaster.

"Second prize," said the boy.

"Darius Bagley!" shouted Nat angrily, her words lost as the stuck children started wailing again.

"He's busy," shouted a voice from the kitchen. "He's seeing how many baked beans he can get up his nose." A chant started up — "One more bean, one more bean!"

Something blew up outside and Nat reckoned it could have been any number of things. She hoped it was Dad. This mess was ALL HIS FAULT. She wondered if she could change schools. Or country.

A cheer rose up from the kitchen. Darius came up the stairs, dripping in beans and tomato sauce. He looked like he had an outbreak of the plague. He held up the empty tin in triumph.

Nat walked over to him, furious. He pulled a stupid 'I'm sorry' face. She tried to be angry with him but couldn't. He looked too funny. He smiled and beans slid down his nose. He caught them with his tongue and ate them. Then he burped a massive beany burp. Nat laughed. She heard a car door slam outside.

"Oh no," she said. "Parents are coming back. They're gonna go mental."

"Who cares?" said Darius as they ran outside across the smouldering wrecks of the garden. "Everyone says this was the best party ever."

Nat's mouth fell open. She looked round. Every mad, whooping, sugar-crazed, manic, bonkers kid did look totally, utterly, deliriously… happy.

And by the look on the parents' faces, Nat thought she might get the best birthday present OF ALL TIME. Surely Dad would get chucked off the committee now? Even HE couldn't get away with this. Could he?

CHAPTER TWENTY-ONE

. . . .

HOWEVER, JUST A FEW DAYS LATER...

"How did the committee meeting go, Dad?" said Nat, lying smugly on the sofa with Mum, scoffing prawn crackers.

She'd had a brilliant couple of days at school, mainly because all the parents had forbidden their kids to play with 'the terrible Bumhole girl'. Which meant of course, for the first time EVER, she was actually very nearly cool. She knew it wouldn't last, but neither did Christmas; it was still great.

And now Dad was off the committee. So he wouldn't be coming into school any more, or running stupid trips, and he DEFINITELY wouldn't be doing a disco!

She had waited up all evening to hear Dad's fate on the POGS. Mum, pretending to read a magazine, chuckled quietly. Without looking up she said, "So? Did they chuck you off?"

"There was a vote TRYING to chuck me off, yes," said Dad. "Something about me being a danger or a menace or something. I can't remember the exact words. But I know you'll both be delighted to hear that in the end the vote was overturned."

Dad beamed.

Nat choked on her prawn crackers. "What? How? WHY?"

"Dolores – that's Miss Hunny to you, Nat – had the deciding vote. She was very good. She said it wasn't fair to judge me on Nat's party as that wasn't an official school affair."

Nat put a squidgy cushion on her head in despair.

"How is little Marcus Milligan, by the way?" said Mum, meaning the boy who bounced into a tree.

"Out of hospital days ago," said Dad brightly. "He didn't break himself too much at all." Mum shook her head. "The air ambulance got him out of that tree very quickly," added Dad. "They're very good. Although the pilot did say I should give him a few days' advance warning the next time I organised anything, which I thought was rude. Cuppa?"

Dad pottered about in the kitchen for a few minutes. He started singing. Badly.

"We probably shouldn't tease your dad QUITE so much," said Mum, smiling at Dad's song-mangling efforts. "Everyone had a brilliant time at your party, which was the whole point of it. And both our neighbours have put their houses up for sale and I never liked them very much."

Nat peeked out from under the cushion.

"Thing is," continued Mum, "no matter how

irritating or annoying or embarrassing he is, I can't stay angry with him very long. He always makes me laugh."

"I know," said Nat. "It's like Darius."

"Annoying, isn't it?" said Mum. "I guess we're stuck with them."

"Although Miss Hunny still hasn't managed to get Darius out of that class and back into mine," said Nat.

Then she grinned to herself. Darius was bringing in his one-legged pet frog tomorrow. A couple of older girls she didn't like were *terrified* of frogs.

Dad came in with tea. "There're no biscuits," he said.

"Yeah, Nan was here," said Nat.

"I'm going to have to break some bad news to the committee though," Dad went on. "Kerri, Bonehead and Cabbage can't do your school disco."

It was all Nat could do to stop herself from punching the air in triumph. She had been dreading Dad arranging the end of term disco, as she knew he would never be able to resist getting on stage and making a total spanner of himself. But now, with his 'celebrity' friends unavailable, there was NO WAY the school would let him organise anything like a disco. *For every cloud...* she thought.

"Why can't they do it?" Nat asked, just wanting to be sure they wouldn't change their minds.

"Kerri got fired for prank-calling the Prime Minister and telling him she'd found his cat run over by a steamroller. She asked if she should just put a stamp on it and post it back to him."

"It's not often you hear the leader of a country sob on live radio," said Mum. "Bonehead's still missing on his charity swim up the Limpopo river," continued Dad, "and Cabbage packed it all in to become an estate agent."

"Poor Cabbage," said Mum.

"There is some good news though," Dad

added, swigging his tea.

Nat held her breath, and prayed…

"I managed to persuade the committee to have a quiz night at school, just as long as I agreed not to actually run it. I thought that was a bit mean, but still, it should be fun. And if it all goes well, who knows, maybe they'll let me do the disco after all."

At the words 'quiz night', Nat stiffened like a cat whose fur has been rubbed the wrong way by a person they don't like, who was wearing a glove made of dog.

"Urgh, I hate quizzes," she said.

"But you like facts," argued Dad.

Nat reluctantly admitted this was true. She quite liked facts. She just didn't like Dad's ideas.

"You'll be even more pleased when you hear I made you a team captain."

"WHAT?" yelled Nat.

"I still have a bit of influence," said Dad smugly.

Mum chuckled into her tea. "See," she said.

"Your dad always makes me laugh. Told you."

"But I won't know the answers," Nat complained. "And it's in front of the whole school!"

"Not just the school," said Dad proudly. "I'm selling tickets around town." Nat buried her head in her hands.

"Anyway," said Dad, "you don't have to know *all* the answers. You'll have a team. And because you're captain, you get to pick your team members. I thought you'd be pleased!"

"I'm the OPPOSITE of pleased," she shouted.

"But being team captain is the thing the cool kids do, right?"

"No, Dad, being football team captain is the thing the cool kids do, not spoddy quizzes. That's just for swots and show-offs."

"If you're team captain, you can pick Darius and show everyone how clever he is," said Mum thoughtfully. "If he's as smart as you say he is, then show the whole school. Maybe get him back to your class."

Nat and Dad stared at Mum in awe.

"Mum, you're a genius," said Nat. "Why couldn't I have got your brains instead of Dad's?" said Nat.

"Sorry about that," said Dad, "but on the bright side, you got your Mum's pretty face."

Dad spent the rest of the night NOT being told off.

CHAPTER TWENTY-TWO

····

AT BREAK NEXT DAY, AFTER DARIUS AND HOPPY the lopsided frog had chased soppy Trudy Merriweather around Mr MacAnuff's organic vegetable plot enough times, Nat told Darius about her plan for the quiz. Nat wasn't worried he'd say no because Darius never said no to anything.

Then she asked Miss Hunny to be on her team. She didn't think Miss Hunny was that clever, but she was the only person in the universe who could make Darius sit still.

But now Nat had a problem. Quiz rules said she needed a pupil, teacher and parent on her team. Which parent to choose? The obvious choice was Dad. Dad loved quizzes, but was properly rubbish at them. Her favourite Dad answers to quiz questions were:

Q: What is created when you boil a kettle?
DAD: a hot kettle.

Q: Where are the Andes?
DAD: At the end of your wristies.

Q: What do you call a tribe in the desert who travel all the time?
DAD: Gonads.

Sometimes she thought Dad said these things just to make her laugh, but in reality she suspected he was probably just plain daft. Either way, there was no way she was going to pick Dad and have another disaster on her hands. And she couldn't ask Mum either because Mum got very cross when people asked her too many questions.

Nat was sitting in maths measuring angles badly and missing Darius when she had a new and even more brilliant idea. She looked at the back of Flora Marling's blonde, perfect head, bent over her textbook. She knew just who to ask.

She got her chance in the games changing rooms that afternoon. Flora Marling's boot laces came undone as they were trotting out on to the wet playing fields. Not noticing they had lost their leader, her minions ran on, leaving Flora Marling briefly alone. As she bent down to tie her laces, Nat made a beeline for her.

"You want my dad to go on a quiz team - with Darius Bagley and Miss Hunny?" Flora replied after a thoughtful pause. "He'd be totally shown up. They're both complete dimwits. My father would look like a total muppet."

Nat felt her face going red yet again, and looked for a nearby hole to crawl into. "He has degrees from Oxford, Cambridge, Harvard, Yale, the Sorbonne and Ulan Bator," recited Flora. "He'd be totally humiliated." Nat, twisting the toe of her boot into the soft grass, was about to mutter an apology when Flora Marling broke into a huge grin. "It sounds brilliant. I'll make sure he says yes."

She trotted off just as the sun broke through the clouds. A wet clod of earth smacked Nat on the back of her head and Nat chased Darius triumphantly round the running track until they were both given detentions.

"The Massive Brains Massive."

"No."

"The Champion Bounty Hunter Manga Question Force."

"No way." There were only a few days to go before the quiz and Darius and Nat were throwing pennies at a wall round the back of the science block one break time. The one who got nearest took the other person's penny. The game was officially banned but no one was watching. Darius tried again. "The Eat My Answer Quiz Doom Die, Losers, Die."

Nat went over and scooped up two pennies. "I am not calling my quiz team The Eat My Answer Quiz Doom Die, Losers, Die. It's stupid."

"You're stupid."

"No, you're stupid."

"You're *both* stupid for playing this game when there are teachers about," said Mr MacAnuff, appearing from behind a bush. He was wearing his vest again, along with cut-off jeans, and had been wandering around outside Miss Hunny's window trying to catch her attention.

"You're not a teacher," said Darius calmly.

Mr MacAnuff hissed like a steam pudding. "Say that again…" he said, in a dangerous voice.

"You're not a teacher," said Darius, saying it again.

"I'm more of a teacher than YOU," replied the caretaker, a bit childishly, in Nat's opinion. "Come with me now, or I will report you to the Head."

Neither Nat or Darius could argue with that, so they followed him all the way to his prized lawn. Neither of them could see anything wrong with it. But Mr MacAnuff was definitely looking at *something*.

"Cock's foot," he said savagely.

Nat and Darius looked at each other.

"He's finally cracked," whispered Darius. "It's because his vest is too tight. Cut off the blood supply to his brain. He's gone mad…"

Nat giggled.

The caretaker gave Darius a stare of pure evil, and carried on. "Creeping Bent. Onion Crouch." The man's face darkened as he hissed, "Yorkshire fog."

"I think I'd rather have a detention," whispered

Nat to Darius, a little alarmed.

"Weeds," said Mr MacAnuff, handing them tiny, tiny garden forks. "Always weeds. Waiting to pop up and strangle the life out of The Lawn. Anything that doesn't look like a blade of grass – kill it."

Darius liked the sound of that and set to work immediately. Nat sighed and snatched up a tiny fork.

They worked together for a while in silence, then Nat saw Darius stop. He was staring at a bunch of bigger boys jostling each other near Mr MacAnuff's shed. They had seen Darius and were shouting things at him. Not very nice things. She was used to being teased because of her name, but this seemed much nastier. This was vicious.

The biggest kid was a mean-looking boy Nat knew was called Wayne Garvey. He was smacking his fist into his palm. "Coming back for some more?" he shouted. From behind his shed, Mr MacAnuff told Wayne to get lost. Nat didn't think Mr MacAnuff sounded quite as brave as when he was telling her and Darius off. Finally Garvey and his equally unpleasant-looking mates sloped off, laughing and spitting on the grass.

"How is it in that new class?" Nat asked quietly.

Darius stabbed a weed savagely. "It's all right," he said.

Nat didn't believe him and just hoped her quiz idea paid off. They worked on in silence till the bell went and they both trudged back inside.

"How's your general knowledge coming on?" asked Dad that night.

"I'm busy," said Nat. She was sprawled on the sofa. She had the TV remote in her left hand, flicking. She was playing her DS with her right hand and had an earphone from her iPod shoved in her left ear. With Darius, Miss Hunny and Mr Doctor Marling on her team, she knew she could sit back and let them do the answering for anything she didn't know. Easy.

Dad raised an eyebrow.

Nat took her earphone out and tapped an encyclopaedia that she'd been pretending to read. "Good," said Dad. "Don't forget the individual round."

Nat looked at him in shock. "You said it was a team game," she said.

"It is, but the captains have to answer questions on their own, didn't I tell you?"

"WHAT?? No, you did not! Test me, test me," she said, panicking.

"What's an alkali?" Dad asked. "Someone from the Middle East?" she answered wrongly.

"What's the capital of Spain?" asked Dad.

"Del Monte," said Nat quickly.

"Hmmm, not quite right, love. Still, don't worry, those questions won't come up," said Dad.

Nat jumped on him and grabbed his head in her hands. "You KNOW what the questions are?" she demanded.

"Not KNOW exactly," he said, squirming,

"but I've got Eric from the Nelson's Arms to do the quiz mastering and he does tend to use the same questions every week. The regulars don't mind because they always get everything right and it impresses everybody else."

"You have to tell me the answers, Dad, I'm SERIOUS. You just have to."

"That's cheating."

"It'll help Darius," she said craftily. "I'll show him the answers too."

"I don't think you'll need to," said Dad. "Miss Hunny thinks he's so bright he's off the scale."

"I'll show them to Miss Hunny then – she's thick."

"No, she's not. She was on *University Challenge.*"

This was getting worse. Nat was set to be properly shown up. She had one more card to play. It was embarrassing, it was humiliating, but she had no choice.

"Dad. Do you want me – your little girl – to sit there, in front of ALL THOSE PEOPLE and be shown up as a complete idiot? You'll look like a bad dad."

Dad looked worried.

Nat knew he hated being thought of as a bad dad. "It'll look like you never did any homework with me, and we just sit around eating pork pies on toast, playing top trumps and watching comedy programmes." Dad looked sick. Nat cunningly had just described Dad's idea of a perfect evening.

"Or worse," she said, warming to the topic now she realised she was winning, "they'll think you don't do any homework with me because *you go to the pub all the time*."

Dad went to the pub exactly once a week, on a Tuesday. He only went to see his mates Monkey Dave and Posh Barry and he only had a couple of pints but he still felt guilty about it because Nathalia made him feel guilty about it. Wednesday morning she would always say things like, "How's your head?" or "What time did you crawl back last night, then?" or even

"You know I can't go to sleep until I hear you're home safely."

"All right," he said, giving in. "There's a quiz night at the pub next week. I suppose I could bring the questions home." Nat clapped her hands in joy. "But I'm not telling you the answers," he said uncomfortably. "That would be cheating."

Thanks to Dad being such a soft touch, this was going to be a doddle…

CHAPTER TWENTY-THREE

••••

I T WAS THE NIGHT OF THE QUIZ, AND THE HALL WAS full. The teams were assembling on the stage and Nat was looking and feeling confident. *Even Dad couldn't ruin tonight*, thought Nat, as they'd only let him help with the sound, on the grounds he couldn't do much harm there. A screech of deafening feedback rang out across the hall. Three hundred people clapped their hands over their ears in agony.

"This quiz is such a bold and exciting event for the school," the Head was saying to the

Chairman of the Governors, from their reserved seats at the front.

"Blooming barmy," shouted the Chair over the feedback. "I don't know what the man's thinking about, trying to bring together people at school like this. It'll never work."

Just then, Mr Kitkat the bearded drama and media teacher came over to them. "I've fixed up the video camera," he said. "We can put it up on the school's website tomorrow."

"That reminds me," said the Chair, raising his voice more loudly. "I tried to get on to the website yesterday."

Nathalia, on stage with her team-mates, was now shouting instructions at Dad. The Chair shouted louder still as the feedback got worse.

"I just got a message that read 'I am the champion bounty hunter, die, losers, die' and a video of a dancing bare backside. My wife saw it and had to lie down."

"We've taken the website down and we're holding a full investigation," said the Head.

"What? Can't hear you above that awful noise," said the Chair. "What you should do of course is compare bottoms. The culprit's bottom is out there. You should line everyone up and see which one matches."

Mrs Trout frowned. "What?" she said.

Darius hopped off the stage, flicked a couple of switches and the howling noise stopped, just as the Chair yelled,

"Bottoms. I want to see bottoms."

There was a horrible silence. Everyone turned towards him. The Chair glared at Darius.

"Tell Ivor to get a move on," said the Head, changing the subject. "I don't like the look of this crowd."

She had a point. Dad had suggested the quiz thinking it would bring cooperation to the school but in reality it had just brought *competition*. Which, as Nat had tried to tell him, brings out the worst in most people. There were four teams competing in the quiz, and they all wanted to win. And all the teams had friends and family in the audience – and they wanted them to win too. It was like putting four rival football teams in one stadium and chucking in a ball. Most sensible referees would then run away, really fast.

Mr Kitkat the bearded drama and media teacher turned on the video camera and got close-ups of the teams. Nat saw it was about to begin and put her hand in her pocket nervously. Her fingers closed round the bit of paper with her answers on. Last night, Dad had given her Eric the Quizmaster's questions just as he had promised, and she'd carefully looked up all the answers. She felt fully quizzed up. A tiny part of her – like, a hair's worth – felt a bit cheaty, but the massive rest of her was pretty relieved, especially as she looked at the opposition.

At last it was time to introduce the teams. Team One, *The Quiz Park Rangers*, was made up of Mr MacAnuff, who was delighted to have confirmed with this place on the team that he was, in fact, a teacher, if only according to Eric the Quizmaster; Marcus Milligan, whose arm was still in plaster after trampolining into the tree at Nat's party; Mr Fletcher, the father of nut-allergy boy Stanley; and Trixie Merriweather, the girl tormented by Darius's frog. All four of them, for their own reasons, were glowering at Nat and Darius. This contest was getting *personal*.

Team two, *Quizzie Rascal*, starred Miss Austen, Penny Posnitch, Penny's friend Abi, and a Mrs Ethers, one of the few parents from the POGS committee who thought Dad was creative and funny and not an utter menace, though now, deafened by the feedback earlier, she was having second thoughts.

Team three, *Quiz Teama Aguilera*, featured a sniffy Miss Eyre, a nervous Mrs Posnitch and two boys who had been best friends ever since Darius glued them together.

Miss Hunny, Nat, Darius and Mr Doctor Marling made up team four. Darius had written down their name on the team sheets as *The Test Icicles*, but at the last minute Miss Hunny had realised what it sounded like, crossed it out and had cleverly written *Universally Challenged*, which even Nat admitted was pretty good.

Finally, Dad handed over to Eric the Quizmaster. Eric was an elderly man with a wrinkled, weather-beaten, beetroot face, who wore a lot of tweed. Everything about him was tweed, from his hat to his socks. Even his face looked like it was woven from tweed. His voice had a tweedy quality to it too, sort of soft and scratchy at the same time.

"We're going straight into round one," Eric said nervously. He wasn't used to this size of audience. He dropped his questions and bent to pick them up. Darius made a rude noise with his eyeball socket and the audience laughed. Eric the Quizmaster straightened up. "It wasn't me," he shouted, which just made people laugh more.

Nat wasn't paying attention. She was thinking fast, thoughts racing, her hand clutching her cheaty answers. She hadn't seen Darius all day to remind him of her plan. She needed to be sure he realised that this was his big chance. He HAD to behave himself and answer the questions properly. These days at break times he just vanished. She had a horrible feeling he was hiding from Wayne Garvey and the other nasty kids in his class.

The four teams were now all ready, sitting behind their tables, in a big semicircle. Someone dimmed the lights and the audience went, "Oooooh!" Then the lights went out altogether, and the audience went, "Booooo!"

"Shall I press this button again?" said Dad. "NO!" shouted everyone in the hall.

"Oy, chimp," whispered Nat, "don't forget, if you do well here, they might realise you're not a total moron after all and move you from that horrible class. So read these, just in case!" She shoved her answers at Darius under the desk. Darius shoved them back at her. "I'll be fine," he said, going back to playing with his chair.

"Don't be so ungrateful," said Nat, "I got these especially for you." She knew that wasn't

ENTIRELY true but she'd very nearly convinced herself it was.

Doctor Marling leaned over, looking annoyed. "What are you two whispering about?" he said. "We're a team. We need to all work together." He grabbed the buzzer. "By the way, I should be team captain. Did I tell you I'm a doctor?"

"That's nice," said Miss Hunny, her sweet voice suddenly edged with steel. "And I suppose you were in the winning team on *University Challenge*?"

Mr Marling said nothing, but said nothing VERY LOUDLY.

"I thought not," she said happily, taking the buzzer. "If anything, I should be captain."

Nat took the buzzer smugly. Now she was here, she was going to do this properly. "I think you'll find that I'M captain, cos it's my dad's quiz," she said. "So you can both get lost."

"Round one!" said Eric the Quizmaster, and the competition began.

Round one was the captains' round. *Straight*

in at the deep end, thought Nat. She began to feel worried as the questions came closer to her. She didn't remember any of them. She had a head full of names and dates and chemical formulas and capital cities but these questions were all really *trivial*. All about films and plays and actors and pop songs and TV shows. Finally it was her turn. Eric looked down at his questions. Perhaps *this* would be about Henry VIII's third wife or the Battle of Trafalgar or what a verb was or which metals make tin or what the French for 'house' was, or the other *zillions* of useless facts she'd stuffed into her head.

"Who played Dr Edible in the horror film *The Hills Have Teeth*?"

"What sort of question's that?" said Nat, unable to stop herself.

"It's the question you've got ten seconds to answer," quipped Eric. Eric worked behind a screen at the post office and told people they had the wrong forms and would they go to the back of the queue and start again, and liked being bossy and so was beginning to enjoy himself. Nat now hated him. People in the audience laughed. Nat felt herself going redder than Eric's nose. She stared out into the sea of faces in the hall, looking angrily for Dad. HE got her into this.

"Um...um..." she floundered. She could see the actor – a tall man with a bald head who pulled funny faces even when he was getting munched by aliens – but couldn't think of his name.

"Tony Mozzarella," whispered Darius.

How the heck did Darius know that? She knew he never went to the cinema. Or maybe he was just guessing...

"Three... Two..." Eric was counting down. Nat could see Mr MacAnuff counting down too. He looked pleased his team had got their answer right.

Nat decided to take a chance. "Tony Mozzarella," she said, expecting a massive roar of laughter.

"Correct!"

On her next turn, it happened again. Eric

asked, "Who was the host of the TV show *When Cats Go Bad*?" Nat floundered. Darius whispered the answer.

"Molly Banjax," repeated Nat. "Correct!" said Eric. Nat was gobsmacked. She knew Darius was clever, but an expert on film and TV too?

The questions came round to her again and the same thing happened a third time. Once again, Nat didn't recognise the question, once again Darius whispered the answer, and once again it was correct! She should have been pleased, but these surprise questions were giving her a sense of impending doom. She had been given THE WRONG QUESTIONS. She looked murderously for Dad, but he was still fiddling with the sound mixer.

It seemed like that was it for the captains' round at least. Now it was the picture round. Teams had to identify objects from weird, close-up photos that were flashed up on a screen by bearded drama and media teacher- Mr Kitkat.

Darius was fastest on the buzzer every time.

"A monkey wrench."

"An electric guitar."

"A space shuttle."

He didn't say bum, willy, boobypants, bogey or anything like that, not even when the pictures looked a bit like a bum, willy, boobypant or bogey. Nat beamed at him with pride. She saw Mr MacAnuff shooting death stares at Darius, and grumbling and muttering to the others on his team. Nat was delighted. Her genius plan was working!

The next round was the knockout round. Two teams were going out. Each team was given ten questions about one topic and they were allowed to discuss before answering. Mr MacAnuff's team got Books. They scored eight out of ten.

The *Quizzie Rascals* had a disastrous round. They got History and only scraped a feeble four points. Miss Austen and her team knew little about the Spanish Armada, not much about the First World War and nothing at all about Alfred the Great, who may as well have been called

Alfred The Totally Unheard Of.

Quiz Teama Aguilera fared slightly better with Sport. Miss Eyre and Mrs Posnitch were pretty good tennis players and the two glued boys knew their football. They scored a solid seven. They thought they might have done enough to get through to the final.

Now it was Nat's team's turn. Nat was desperately hoping the topic would be Science because she'd spent hours trying to remember trillions of pointless science factoids. She could now label all the parts of the body AND all the parts of an internal combustion engine. She knew which planet came after Jupiter and which element came after Helium. She'd actually remembered whilst swotting up that she really did like facts, even when it was Dad's fault that she had to learn them.

"The subject is flowers," said Eric the Quizmaster.

"Arrrrgh nooo!" said Nat, too loudly. People tittered. Nat simmered in quiet rage. That was

IT. Dad was going to suffer for this. She looked over at Mr Doctor Marling, who was also clearly alarmed. He shrugged. "I can't tell a rose from a rhododendron," he said. Nat looked over at Miss Hunny but she was shaking her head. "I had some flowers once, but they died," she moaned. They were *doomed*. Unless...

Darius answered all ten questions correctly. He knew what country dandelions came from, the colour of a Tudor rose and the date of National Flower Day in Azerbaijan (May 10th). He even knew the Latin name for Giant Hogweed although missed out on the bonus point for not being able to spell it. The audience clapped like mad, as Darius took a small bow. Mr MacAnuff was practically jumping up and down with anger. Nat could see him mouthing the words "...must be cheating, must be cheating..."

There was a short break to add up the total scores. Darius's team-mates turned to him in amazement. Miss Hunny was thrilled. "I knew there was more to you than... well, you," she said. She was going to hug him but his jumper was glistening with various substances and she changed her mind.

"How are you doing this?" whispered Nat, as Eric the Quizmaster returned to the podium with the scores.

"I've been in the library all week, where you should have been. I didn't want you to look like an idiot," Darius said simply.

WHAT? He didn't want HER to look like an idiot?? Suddenly Nat was ABSOLUTELY FURIOUS. Here she was trying to save him, and he had the cheek to try and save HER? "I'm never speaking to you again," she said. "You... git."

When the scores were read out, *Quizzie Rascal* and *Quiz Teama Aguilera* were eliminated. Now it was a straight shoot-out between Nat's team and Mr MacAnuff's, in the final. It was going to be a grudge match. The audience were starting to take sides. Quite a few people thought Darius must be cheating, while others said that was sour grapes and they should stop their moaning. A minor scuffle broke out after Dad accidentally turned all the lights out again and no one could see who was jabbing who in the ribs.

The final was a close-fought affair, questions coming thick and fast. It was a free-for-all, with fastest fingers on the buzzers getting to shout out the answer. Time counted down; it was close, very close. Mr Doctor Marling was great at science, Miss Hunny was a whizz at poetry, but against them, Mister MacAnuff was red-hot on beer and daytime TV.

The contest was even closer than it should have been because Nat wouldn't let their star team member answer any questions. She didn't care how stupid she looked, every time he buzzed, she butted in before Darius could answer.

"What are you doing, girl?" said Mr Doctor Marling, after Nat had suggested that the first names of the three Brontë sisters were TinkyWinky, La-La and Po.

"Let Bagley answer," he said, frustrated. "He's

quite clearly a damn sight smar_

That was IT. That made Nat

MORE ANGRY. He was – but why did _

have to be so sure of it? Now she just buzz_

every question, whether she had any idea of the

answer or not. She was just shouting out random

answers to all the pointless questions she'd been

forced to learn by her STUPID DAD. They

didn't match the questions. Worse, this was the

very final round, where Eric took points away

for wrong answers.

"Stop it," said Darius, after Nat put the Sea of

Tranquillity in Africa rather than on the moon

where it belonged. "I know all the answers."

"How? How have you remembered all this

– even with the library to help you? Because

you're just sooo clever?" she hissed back.

"Well, yes," he said, "and because my brother

makes me watch a lot of TV."

But it didn't matter now. Nat couldn't control

herself.

Nat's team saw their lead slip as Nat got

question after question wrong. Finally, Mr Doctor Marling and Miss Hunny grabbed her hands to stop her pressing the buzzer. The audience cheered as Nat wriggled, frantically trying to get free. She even tried to buzz with her forehead, banging her head on the desk. The audience applauded. "Don't clap at that," shouted Dad.

Nat heard the laughter from the crowd.

Across the tables, Penny Posnitch was looking at her and mouthing: "Shut up, shut up, shut up."

But it was too late to stop now.

"Costa Rica," she shouted. "Wolverhampton Wanderers."

The audience were really glad they'd come to see this. Even the Chair was thoroughly enjoying himself. "I have to admit," he said to the Head, "since that idiot took over the POGS committee, evenings at school have been much more fun." The Head sighed.

Nat was still yelling. "*Treasure Island*. Queen Victoria. A fruit bat." The bell went and Eric started to add up the scores.

Nat took deep breaths. "I hope you're pleased with yourself," she said to Darius.

"How dare you try to help me when I'm trying to help you."

"Friends help EACH OTHER, Buttface," said Darius.

Oh... poo, thought Nat. *He's right. Bum, willie, poo.* She was mortified – she'd done exactly the opposite of what she'd meant to do. He was her friend and she was meant to be saving him, not exacting revenge!

"It's a tie," shouted Eric.

"Ooooh," went the audience.

"Tie break!" shouted Mr MacAnuff, who would show Bagley who was a non-teacher. "Let's see who's the best."

"Oooooh," said the audience again. With an extra 'o' this time.

"Good idea," said Eric. Each team had to pick one member to go head-to-head to answer a tie-break question. "It's obviously me or the Bagley," said Mr Doctor Marling.

"Let Darius do it," said Nat.

Miss Hunny looked at Mr Doctor Marling. "We

should encourage children," she said. "Go on, Darius."

Darius shrugged, and took the buzzer.

Mr MacAnuff took his team's buzzer, eyeballing Darius evilly.

The whole room was silent, waiting for the question.

"Who has dug the word 'Darius' into Mister MacAnuff's prize lawn?" shouted the wife of the Chair, Mrs Thin-and-ugly, who had got bored and gone for a walk.

"WHAAAT?" said Mr MacAnuff, jumping off the stage and running out.

"Do we win?" asked Nat.

"I don't care," said the Quizmaster. "But I need a drink."

CHAPTER TWENTY-FOUR

• • • •

NAT WAS MISERABLE AS SHE CLAMBERED INTO THE Atomic Dustbin after school the next day. Darius had been suspended, while the evil lawn crime was being investigated. She'd overheard Miss Hunny arguing with Miss Austen outside the staff room. Miss Hunny seemed really upset and was saying stuff about "innocent until proved guilty". Afterwards, Nat was going to ask her if she was all right, but then she remembered how the teacher had nearly ruined her life by being friends with Dad, so didn't.

"What's going to happen to him, Dad?" asked Nat as they drove to school.

Dad didn't answer for a while. Finally he said: "Your school think he's trouble but they're wrong." There was an angry tone in Dad's voice that Nat didn't hear very often. He looked furious. "And I don't think he dug his name into that stupid lawn. For a start, 'Darius' was spelled properly. I've seen his writing. Even when he does get the letters in the right order, he puts most of them backwards."

"Good point, Dad," said Nat, impressed.

"The poor kid might stand a chance if he had parents who could talk to the Head about it, but Darius has only got Oswald."

Nat didn't say anything – she knew what that meant. "He's got me too, Dad," she said.

"Good girl," he said proudly. "I wish I had friends like you."

"Yeah," said Nat, remembering Dad's rubbish mates, the former DJs, "yours let you down."

Dad smiled gently, also remembering his

rubbish mates. "*They* might, but the important thing is, not to let THEM down."

Nat thought about Darius and wondered what she could do.

"Which reminds me, I know what'll cheer you up," said Dad. Nat started to worry. "Because of my quiz-night triumph, they're letting me do a disco after all."

"No – no, you can't…" stammered Nat.

"Ah, you're thinking I haven't got the DJ's. Well, I found a replacement."

"Who?" Nat asked nervously.

"Oh, he's very good," said Dad in a voice that warned Nat something horrid was about to happen. "He dope."

"Who's a dope?" she said, growing more suspicious.

"Only the Wolverhampton wizard of the wheels of steel, the vinyl villain in Da House…"

This was SO bad news. "Oh no, Dad…"

Dad started rapping. "Oh no, Dad, that's what they tell us – but that's cos the other DJs is getting jealous..."

"Please, Dad, no, I'll do anything, I'll eat my spinach and do my homework..."

"My homework, going beserk... can't think of another rhyme for homework."

Nooooo. Dad was going to do the disco himself. AAAAAARGH.

"I'm doing the disco myself," explained Dad, unnecessarily.

"Please don't," said Nat. "For a start, all your records are rubbish." Dad stopped rapping. He thought about this for a minute. "They are quite rubbish," he admitted. "I mean, *I* like them but I'm not sure anyone else does. To be perfectly honest, I've even got records that the bands who made the records don't like."

"So that's the first reason I'm not going."

Dad looked disappointed. "Have a bit of faith, love," he said. "I can get up to date with modern music. I'll even listen to Radio Two."

"And that's the second reason I'm not going. But the main reason is I don't want to watch you up on stage dancing about with headphones on, rapping and waving a glow-stick."

"But I can't cancel the disco, I've already printed up all the tickets," said Dad, who very much planned to dance about on stage rapping and waving a glow-stick. "I can't let everyone down." Dad rubbed his head and made the first discovery of what was to become The Bald Spot That Must Never Be Mentioned.

"It'll be a disaster, Dad." Surprisingly, this stopped him.

"Oh," he said, suddenly unsure. "That's actually a good point. They said one more disaster and I'll be chucked off the committee for life. We don't want that, do we?"

This stopped Nat. She DID want this. She wanted it a lot. Evil Nat started twirling her evil moustache. So Dad was *only one more disaster away*, was he? Right. Perhaps it was worth one final burst of utter humiliation and shame. No pain, no gain.

"No, you should *definitely* do the disco," she

said craftily. "You can't let people down. You're right. Bring all your favourite records." This was it. Goodbye, Dad. Three hours of the Electric Meerkats and the Exploding Bongo Band and he'd be out of school for good. Like Darius. *Darius…*

"GENIUS IDEA ALERT!" shouted Dad so loudly that Nat almost jumped out of her seat and a nearby cyclist fell off his bike. "Darius isn't suspended from the disco, is he? No, he's not. He can help me set it up, show that silly school he can behave. Yeah, he can help me download all the modern hits. I might even do some mixing and… whatever it is they do. And he can do some visuals and just generally help me out, and maybe your teachers will see there's more to him than – you know…"

"Burping and farting and twitching and running out of class and terrorising the girls and giving teachers nervous breakdowns?"

"Work with me on this, love."

Nat sighed in agreement. She wanted Darius back and was out of sensible ideas.

Dad arranged for Darius to stay with them until the disco. He said it was so they could work on their show but Nat thought it was really just to get him away from Oswald for a while. Oswald seemed keen to get rid of him when they went to collect him.

Darius was his usual hyper-scratching-twitching-running-jumping-cartwheeling-head-standing-picking-farting-joking self. He made them laugh all the way home, especially when he used the Dog as a ventriloquist dummy and told a rude story about bumsniffs. The Dog didn't care what Darius did, he just liked licking him. He always found something tasty.

As it turned out, Darius was even better at the computer than Dad had hoped. By the end of the first night at their house, and with the help of Dad's credit card, Darius had set up a virtual DJ booth, complete with 'banging' tunes, 'rad' beats and a 'some other word Dad didn't recognise' lightshow. He'd also set up a bank account under the name of IP FREELY but Dad made him close it down in case he got a dawn raid from the authorities.

The next day even Nat found herself, with Dad and his little helper, in an electronics store hiring a big projector for the night. The idea was to hook this up to his laptop and show videos and animations, to go along with the music. Who needed Kerri, Bonehead and flipping Cabbage? Not Dad and Darius, that was for sure.

This was definitely going to be a school disco that no one would ever forget.

Whether that was going to be a good thing or not, only time would tell. But Nat realised, either way, whether she liked it or not, there was no way she could miss it.

CHAPTER TWENTY-FIVE

. . . .

THE DISCO WAS DUE TO KICK OFF A COUPLE OF HOURS after school on Friday, the last day of term. Mr MacAnuff had been told to decorate the gym, and he'd tried his best, bearing in mind he hadn't been in a disco for ten years. There was a big disco ball, a few coloured lights and lots of bright streamers. Class 7H had made a poster as an art project. It read:

LET'S GO!
DISCO
PRATY.

When Nat pointed out politely that 'Party' is traditionally spelled differently, the art teacher Miss Glossop had told her, rather defensively, Nat thought, that it was an art project not an English project and to mind her own business.

Mr MacAnuff was looking forward to the disco so much that he'd bought a new vest especially. It was even tighter than his usual one. Tonight, he'd decided to ask Miss Hunny out. Her saying yes would take away some of the pain he still felt over his ruined lawn. He reckoned the rest of the pain would be taken away by the fact that he was never going to see Darius Bagley ever again.

In fact he did see Darius again, and a lot sooner than he'd have liked, when the boy came trotting in with Nat and Dad and Mr Kitkat the bearded drama and media teacher. They were all hauling the big projector. Mr MacAnuff glimpsed them through a gym window. He was outside putting up the DISCO PRATY banner and was so angry he almost fell off his ladder.

In the gym, Darius was kept so busy setting

up the electronic gear that he didn't have a chance to be naughty. Mr Kitkat the bearded drama and media teacher looked at Dad in amazement. "Is this the real Darius Bagley?" he asked Dad, after an hour of eyeball fartless eleven-year-old. "I saw a science-fiction film last night about aliens who take over children. They behave really nicely until your back's turned and then they morph into space spiders and eat your face off."

Dad laughed nervously. "That's silly," he said. But neither he nor Mr Kitkat took their eyes off Darius for quite a while after that. Right until a massive, shockingly loud explosion made them both jump. "The invasion's started!" shouted Mr Kitkat, who was a very artistic, imaginative and cowardly sort of chap. He was halfway to hiding under the gym mats before he realised it was just Darius turning up the bass and hitting 'play' on a top-ten tune.

"It works then," shouted Dad, as the tune banged on relentlessly.

"You what?" shouted Darius. "Can't hear you…"

Now they'd sorted the music, Darius went on to sort out the visuals. He fiddled about with the laptop for a while but all that came up on the projector was Dad's screensaver – a nice family photo of him and Mum and Nat and The Dog on a beach. Dad smiled at it. Nat scowled.

"Better take that down," Dad shouted over the music, seeing Nat's face. "She'll never let me hear the end of it."

A few minutes later, Darius managed to get some lovely swirly patterns up, dancing in time to the music. It looked great. Mr Kitkat clapped.

Dad gave Darius the thumbs up. "Now please turn that horrible noise off," he shouted.

Darius cut the power. "Great," said Dad, relieved. "Let's get a can of pop, and some glow-sticks. I'm on soon."

'Soon' came 'too soon' for Nat. The gym was packed. It seemed like most of the school had turned up for the disco. This was probably because Dad had forgotten to tell anyone that

Kerri, Bonehead and Cabbage weren't coming. So there were quite a few groans and boos when he made the announcement that HE was doing the disco-ing. Most of the boos – and all of the bad language – came from the teachers. A lot of them had come hoping to get a photo with the stars.

"It's like a funky tidal wave!" blared Dad, who'd found a microphone and was now hopping about on stage.

Nat cringed. If only Mum could have come, she might have kept Dad from embarrassing her like this, but she was working late AGAIN. Nat was jealous of her mum at times. This was one of those times. However, with a bit of luck Dad would be chucked off the committee before he had a chance to make too big a fool of himself.

"Is that *Darius* up there with your dad?" asked Penny, walking over to Nat. It was a bit hard to see because the lights were so dim. At the far end of the gym there was a raised platform like a little stage, where Dad was going to DJ. A smaller, twitchy figure was up there, tapping on a laptop.

"Yup," said Nat, resigned. "Dad and Darius together. We'll be lucky if the school's still standing in an hour."

Penny brightened at the thought. "We can but hope," she said, before walking off again.

"Ride the funky wave, c'mon!" shouted Dad again, waving his arms about like he was drowning and had spotted a passing lifeboat. He was holding a glow-stick.

Nat wished she hadn't had to come.

No one seemed inclined to ride the wave, no matter how funky. As soon as the music started, all the girls immediately scattered to one side of the gym, all the boys to the other. It was like an invisible snowplough had driven between them. But then the video light show suddenly blazed into life and swirly patterns flared up on the huge screen. People stopped boo-ing. Even Nat had to admit it was rather good. On stage, Dad high-fived Darius.

A few of the older girls edged into the middle of the floor, and with set faces, started dancing. They had come to have a good time and were grimly determined to have one, no matter what sort of idiot was playing the songs.

Darius had chosen the music cleverly, starting with the sort of songs no schoolgirl could resist. Dad had decided to leave the playlist entirely to him and really concentrate on his MCing, and encouraging the crowd to dance.

"I'm going to milk the groove and make some tasty shakes!" boomed Dad the MC, rocking the mic. Nat died a little bit inside.

Some of the teachers laughed. Nat realised they thought that Dad was only *pretending* to be a complete idiot. She wanted to shake them and say, "No! This is what he's really like! He thinks it's good! Make him STOP." A few more girls began dancing and Nat had a horrible feeling that Dad was *getting away with it*.

"Just what is that awful boy doing in here?" asked Miss Eyre, who hadn't got anyone to bring to the disco except Miss Austen and was feeling grumpy about it. She was shouting so loudly Nat overheard every word.

"It's an outrage – he's suspended during our *investigations*," shouted Miss Austen, just as grumpily.

"He doesn't need investigating, he needs *incarcerating*," replied Miss Eyre, pleased with her use of big words.

Nat was crushed. She was fooling herself that the school might take Darius back. So she was putting herself through this humiliation FOR NOTHING. The world was a cold, bleak and unforgiving place of misery and pain. Then she realised she was turning into Bad News Nan. Which only made her MORE miserable.

"I like this one," said Penny, who came dancing up to Nat. "Do you want to dance?"

Nat looked at her in horror. "Are you MAD?" she said, then, losing it a bit, "Can't you see – we're all doomed."

"Tear the roof off! Come for your funky fill,

now you're funking ill!" yelled Dad.

"He's so funny!" said Penny. "Come on, now we're here…"

Nat edged away. "I've… I've gotta go to the loo," she said, and ran out. On the way she saw Mr MacAnuff laughing with Miss Hunny. She didn't like the look on the caretaker's face. He was like a cat who'd cornered a mouse wearing a cream-flavoured hat.

Back on stage, Dad was growing in confidence as the dance floor filled up. He turned to Darius, who was fiddling with something shiny and silvery.

"What's that?" Dad asked.

"A camera," said Darius, who'd stopped fiddling and was looking straight at Dad.

"Brilliant," said Dad. "Great idea. Take my picture waving a glo-stick."

"No," said Darius. "I want to tell you something."

"Is it about riding the funky train?" said Dad, who had boarded it ages ago.

"It's not about riding the funky train."

"Then it'll have to wait until the funky train gets into the station and we all get off and, um…"

Unlike the funky train, Dad was running out of funky steam. "…And we mustn't forget to take all our belongings with us."

Darius had no idea what Dad was going on about. Neither had Dad, but that had never stopped him before. "Then we have to get our funky tickets out at the barriers and er… *then* you can tell me. Look, just play another song, they love us."

Nat waited in the loo for twenty minutes until there was a reasonable chance Dad had finally done something terrible and was being carted out by an angry mob. She popped her head back round the gym doors just in time to hear him shout the two most frightening words in human history.

"Bongo solo!"

Darius cut the music. Dad whipped out his bongos.

"AAAAARRRGH!!!!" screamed Nat. She ran back to the loo, bright red in the face. *Even if they do let Darius back into school* and *make him head boy*, she thought, *it STILL ISN'T WORTH IT.*

A little while later she heard a knock at the cubicle door.

Nat stayed silent, hoping they'd just go away.

"It's Penny. I know you're in there." Nat relented and opened the door.

"Come back," said Penny. "Everyone's having a nice time. Your dad's OK. Really. He's funny."

"He's really not," said Nat miserably, letting herself get marched back to the thundering noise of the disco.

"He just likes making people happy," said Penny.

What about ME, though? thought Nat, who had made up her mind to sulk until she was eighteen or adopted, whichever came first.

The disco was now in full swing. And what a swing. The music was good, the light show was great; against all sane predictions it was heading for success. Both Dad and Darius were rocking. Even the teachers, who had been irritated not to see the three semi-famous DJs, were having fun. And they'd stopped looking at Darius the way people look at their shoes after a walk around a sick donkey refuge.

Nat was beginning to think about hoping things might possibly turn out OK after all.

AND Penny was still talking to her…

Just then, Nat saw Flora Marling effortlessly dancing. Nat felt like a lump. And then Flora smiled at her. From the depths of despair, Nat had wings on her feet. Darius might be saved, Penny might think she's at least OK and Flora Marling SMILED at her.

Nat took a chance and edged slowly on to the dance floor, over towards the smiling, dancing Flora Marling.

"My boring dad wouldn't even dance at his own wedding," Flora shouted. "You're soooo lucky."

Nat looked at her father on stage, hopping about like a baboon on a hot car roof. And she almost smiled.

And then Dad did something that wiped the almost-smile right off her face.

"Is that a *video* camera?" said Dad, noticing the shiny thing Darius was fiddling with. Darius tried to drop it into his bag but Dad grabbed it. "I know why you've got this," said Dad.

Darius looked miserable. "I've tried to tell you…" he began.

"No need," said Dad. "You think we should film the crowd, and show it on the screen, all blown up."

"No, I…" began Darius, but Dad wasn't listening. "Great idea. All the trendy clubs do it. I've seen a lead somewhere – I'll plug the camera into the laptop. Do I press this?"

He jabbed a bunch of buttons, almost at random. OK, entirely at random.

"Welcome to Christmas!" said Dad, incredibly loudly. But it wasn't Dad the Disco King of tonight. It was Dad *on screen*. A huge Dad. A younger Dad. A Dad with hair.

"What did you press?" shouted Darius. "You're playing a video from the hard drive."

"Am I? I don't know. What's happening?" said Dad, immediately panicking when faced with technology out of control.

But Nat knew. She knew what was happening without asking. She recognised the video. She stopped dead in mid-boogie and went stone cold. No, colder than stone. Stone was hot compared to Nat. Nat was colder than an ice cube dropped in a bucket of liquid nitrogen that had been left in a very cold freezer in deep space.

She knew this video. She had seen this video. And worse, far, *far* worse...

She was IN this video.

CHAPTER TWENTY-SIX

••••

For Nat to get to the disco that night, Nice Nat and Evil Villain Nat had had to declare a truce in her little blonde head. They had both agreed to put up with SOME Dad-related embarrassment to get what they wanted. Maybe Darius would be rescued (pleasing Nice Nat) and maybe Dad would get publicly sacked (pleasing Evil Villain Nat).

Some embarrassment, yes. But neither of them, in their worst, their deepest, darkest, most terrifying nightmares, had ever thought *this* might happen.

The huge on-screen younger Dad was chatting happily. He was filming a living room in the chaos of Christmas. *Nat's* living room. Under a sparkling tree, presents lay unwrapped. The real Nat couldn't take her eyes off a younger Mum, smiling in a dressing gown.

"We should probably turn this off," said real Dad, heading back to the stage.

But Mr MacAnuff stood in his way. "Let's see that camera," he said.

"In a minute," said Dad. "I have to sort this out."

But Mr MacAnuff was quicker than Dad. He hopped up on stage and grabbed Darius. "I've got you now!" he said nastily. "A vandal AND a thief."

Meanwhile, the video footage was still running. The crowd of teachers and classmates all watched as a six-metre high baby came on to the screen. A six-metre high, totally NAKED baby.

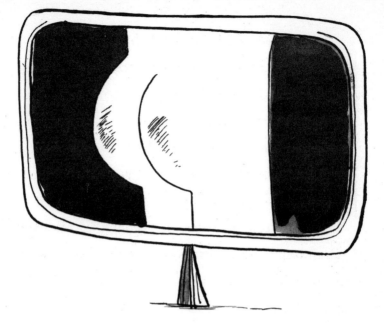

"It's your first Christmas, isn't it?" the younger, on-screen, hairy Dad said. "Yes, it is. Say hello to the world." The baby gurgled and rolled over, showing a big round, bare baby's bum.

Nat's mind was racing. *If he doesn't mention my name I might get away with it*, she thought desperately.

"Don't be shy," said younger Dad, turning over the baby. "It's only Dad. Say hello, NATHALIA BEW-MOLE-AY."

"AAAAARGH!" yelled baby Nat.

"AAAARGH!" yelled eleven-year-old Nat.

"HAHAHAHA!" laughed almost everyone.

"Ow!" yelled Darius.

"He bit me!" yelled Mr MacAnuff.

"Take your hands off him!" yelled Dad.

"DAD, I HATE YOU!"

The words cut through the laughter and the shouting. They were hot words. They were serious. They were *meant*. Darius broke free and paused the music and the video bum.

The gym went deathly quiet.

Mr MacAnuff sucked at his bitten hand. Nat stared at her dad, cold with fury.

"Every day," shouted Nat. "Every day you show me up." Dad looked around for something to distract her with. He was ideally hoping for a puppy to trot past. Nat liked puppies. Or a fluffy kitten. Maybe a puppy *riding* a kitten. Or better yet, a unicorn... But Nat was only standing a few metres away and the look on her face brought him back to reality. He gave her a weak smile.

"I thought you would grow out of it, but no. You've got worse."

Dad now had two thoughts float across his mind as he faced his furious daughter. One – the disco wasn't going quite according to plan and two – how much she looked like her mum, who he missed, rather a lot. He smiled, which was entirely the wrong thing to do.

"Don't you dare laugh at me!"

Dad immediately stopped smiling.

Behind Nat, the ageing laptop now seemed to

be going through all Dad's digital photos. First up on the big projector screen was an old photo of Dad cuddling a five-year-old girl, a little girl with long blonde hair and brown eyes and a button nose who looked nervous on her way to school. The crowd went, "Aaaaah." Nat looked at the picture and something caught in her throat. She stumbled over her words, but then steeled herself as she remembered all of Dad's many crimes.

"Even when I started at this school and asked you REALLY NICELY not to show me up, what did you do? First day, you chased me up a tree dressed as a clown."

"Well, no, it was a *goose* that chased you—"

"But it was YOUR FAULT. Like it was your fault we have to drive round in a horrible old van; your fault we got chucked out of the cathedral and Darius almost got arrested; your fault I had to draw that stupid old ugly man at open evening while everyone watched me; your fault that I'm called Bumhole – yes, it's BUMHOLE Dad; your fault I had to sit on a stage and do a stupid quiz that I didn't know any of the answers to and your fault the school's had a good laugh at me WITH NO CLOTHES ON!"

The crowd all agreed it had been an eventful term.

"Will you ever learn that I don't like being the centre of attention," yelled Nat, very much the centre of attention. Behind her, the photos on the screen kept changing. Most were of Nat and Dad. Birthdays, holidays, funfairs, bike rides, ice creams and picnics. The cake he made in the shape of a pork pie, which she refused to eat because she'd turned veggie that week; Dad looking ill after going on a roller-coaster; Dad chasing after her balloon; Dad getting strangled in her kite strings.

Nat knew that the pictures were there but was trying to ignore them. She had that look of someone who was absolutely sure they were right, and Dad had the guilty look of someone caught with their hand in the biscuit jar. He knew she was right too.

"It was your fault my party became more dangerous than the Battle of Hastings and it's your fault I've come here tonight and THIS happens and now everyone's going to laugh at me for the rest of my life…" There was so much more she could say, but she was exhausted now, and the photos had taken the heat out of her anger.

Miss Eyre turned to Miss Austen. "When she puts it like that, I actually feel sorry for the girl."

"All your fault, Dad." Nat was drained. Her eyes were red, her lips, once firm, were trembling. Even Dad realised he was in trouble. Proper trouble.

Dad walked over to Nat. He put his hand on her shoulder. She pushed it off. He knelt.

"I'm sorry, love," he said.

"Not good enough," she sniffed.

"I try to do what's best for you. I try to cheer you up when you're upset. Admittedly that often makes you more upset, but you know… I tried to help you make friends at your new school and

I try to let everyone see who I see. That you're beautiful and talented and kind and deserve to be happy."

"Stoppit, Dad, you're making it worse," she sniffled.

"I'm leaving the school committee. I don't want to upset you any more. I thought I could make school a bit better for you. I think I made it worse." He looked thoroughly miserable.

"Yeah, you have," said Nat.

A slim, pale hand was placed on her shoulder. She turned. It was Flora Marling, who had been entranced by the happy family photos. "Give him a break," said Flora. Dad looked at her gratefully. "We've ALL got rubbish dads." Dad looked at her a bit *less* gratefully.

"Look at the screen!" shouted Penny Posnitch suddenly.

All the time Nat had been shouting, Darius had been fiddling. No one had taken any notice of him because Darius was always fiddling with something.

But now the pictures of Nat and Dad had disappeared. They'd been replaced by a different video. It was a video taken on the night of the school quiz; random footage filmed by someone who was clearly just walking around the school, filming down corridors, into empty classrooms, and then – out of a window and on to Mr MacAnuff's precious lawn, in all its pre-vandalised green and pleasant glory. The video was shot from a window, high up. It was obviously after school because no one was about.

But now what was this? Caught on the video, two figures ran on to the lawn, looking around furtively. They had spades. They started digging up the turf. The crowd gave an intake of collective breath. The camera zoomed in. It was two of the big lads from Darius's new class. They were caught red-handed, digging out the letters D A R –

"And where do you think you're going?" said Mr Frantz, grabbing the same two lads – Wayne Garvey and one of his nasty little friends – as they tried to sneak out of the gym.

Nat's heart leapt, her misery almost forgotten. Darius was safe!

"He's not out of the woods yet," yelled Mr MacAnuff. "He might have filmed those boys – who will of course be dealt with most severely – but he still stole the school's camera."

It was sort of true.

What Darius explained was this. Before the quiz started, he was helping Mr Kitkat set up the camera so they could film the quiz and put it all up on the website the next day. But he'd 'borrowed' it quickly to film a bit of extra footage. (Darius often did this, as the Chairman of the Governors knew only too well, having seen the video of the infamous dancing bare bottom on the school's website.) Darius had pootled around school videoing stuff until he got bored (which took about forty-five seconds) when he accidentally dropped the camera.

Worried it might be broken, in the confusion following the quiz, Darius pocketed the camera to take home and repair. Darius was good with his hands, and found they got him into less trouble if they were kept busy. It was only then he saw what he'd filmed.

"I couldn't bring it back because you suspended me," he said to the Head, who looked back at him stony-faced.

Darius might have been a bit daft, but he was smart enough to know that literally NO ONE – apart from someone equally daft, like Nat's dad – would believe this story. Even if he showed teachers that he'd actually filmed the vandals, he'd be in EVEN DEEPER TROUBLE for stealing.

He was right. Mr MacAnuff was now looking like a cat who'd given up trying to eat the creamy-hatted mouse because he'd seen a fat rat in a cream bun with catnip on top.

"Never mind suspended," he said, "you stole this and I'm calling the police."

Nat felt sick. Darius was in SERIOUS trouble. The sort of trouble that only something truly amazing, unlikely and incredible could get him out of.

And then Dad did something truly amazing, unlikely and incredible.

He walked up to the stage, looked the caretaker square in the eye and said, "No. Darius is fibbing. *I* borrowed the camera for the disco. I meant to ask but I forgot. I'm very forgetful."

"Don't be an idiot," snarled Mr MacAnuff. "Don't get yourself into trouble for *him*."

Suddenly Nat found herself standing next to Dad. She said, "I can vouch for that too. Dad borrowed it. Darius wouldn't steal." Then, taking a deep breath, she added, "He's my best friend. I should know."

As Nat stood there, she felt someone small slipping their arm through hers. It was Penny Posnitch. She whispered in Nat's ear, "You stuck by your best friend. That's ever so nice. And I'm going to stick by you."

Nat felt a warm glow of pride spreading through her.

"Even if it means I get Darius as well," Penny added with a sigh.

Miss Hunny was looking at the caretaker like she'd suddenly realised he really wasn't very nice after all. Nat tutted – she could have told her that *ages* ago.

"I don't think I'm in trouble," said Dad, who had seen something everyone else seemed to have missed. "Let's just play this video again, shall we?" He rewound and then played the video a few seconds. There was the lawn, the boys, then... a blurry figure could just be seen launching itself across the lawn and starting to chase the boys off just before Darius had swung the camera back round. "I wonder who THAT is?" said Dad.

"Oooh," said the crowd, as the plot thickened.

"It's not me," said Mr MacAnuff too quickly.

"No," said Dad. "It can't have been you, otherwise you'd have known all along that Darius didn't do it. And that would make you really mean." Mr MacAnuff shuffled about awkwardly.

"Oh well," continued Dad, "you said you were calling the police – I'm sure they can get to the bottom of it."

"Oh, no need for them," said the caretaker hastily. "You say you borrowed the camera – I'm sure you had your reasons. No harm done, eh? Best forgotten about. Least said, soonest mended." He held out his bitten hand to Darius. "I suppose it's welcome back," he said through gritted teeth.

Darius looked at the hand, shrugged and bared his own teeth. "Shake it, don't chew it," said Dad.

A few people clapped. Most groaned. Darius was never going to be THAT popular, after all.

Dad felt two little arms wrap round him. It was Nat. He kissed the top of her head and for once she didn't mind who was watching.

"Put the music back on, Darius," said Dad, walking over to him. "I feel like dancing!"

As the thundering bass shook the floor, Mr MacAnuff slunk off back to his potting shed. He couldn't look Miss Hunny in the eye.

Just then a familiar arm slid round Nat's neck. She turned. Her mum stood there, all dressed up in her posh frock. She looked beautiful and glamorous. "I thought you were working!" squealed Nat happily, hugging her.

"I juggled stuff around," said Mum. "You get good at that when you're a girl. It's called multi-tasking."

Tell us about it, thought Nice Nat and Evil Villain Nat – who had somehow BOTH got what they wanted. *We're pooped.*

"Well, I told my new bosses that I'm just going to have to travel a bit less and they'll have to lump it. I wasn't going to miss the fun this time," said Mum.

"Fun? *FUN??*"

"Yeah, you and your big daft dad get to do all the cool stuff. I just get boring work. I'm quite jealous." Nat had never thought of it like that. She hugged Mum tight.

Dad came off the podium. He hugged both of them and they let him. Around them the disco was in full swing. Even the teachers had decided to get, like, *down*. Mr Frantz was dancing like only a German maths teacher who hadn't danced for twenty years can dance. Miss Hunny was in Boogie Wonderland with the new Spanish supply teacher. The Head was tapping her feet and wondering what half the words in this song were and just exactly *how* rude it was. Miss Glossop the art teacher was doing some kind of free-form mad jazz limbo and Misses Eyre and Austen both had sour faces and their fingers in their ears.

Nat looked up at Darius, who was dropping beats with one hand and doing something disgusting with the other.

"Nice one, Buttface," said Darius.

"Nice one, chimpy," said Nat.

Penny beckoned her to dance. "I like this one," she shouted. "No one's realised how rude it is yet." Abi and Frankeee smiled at her too. Not laughed at, *smiled at*.

"Off you go," said Dad, finally releasing her.

He looked Nat straight in the eye. "I'll never embarrass you again," he fibbed. She grinned up at the big idiot.

"I believe you, Dad," she fibbed back.

And with that, she went off to join her friends.

More from

Nathalia BUTTFACE

Coming soon!
And here's a sneak preview...

It was the Saturday after school finished and Nat and Dad were outside the house, packing the Atomic Dustbin ready for their holiday. This involved first *un*packing the Atomic Dustbin, as it was always full of junk. It was crammed with the stuff Dad liked that Mum wouldn't let in the house. So anyone walking past their drive that morning would have seen a rubbish van parked next to a rubbish tip. Nat had a baseball cap pulled down as far over her face as possible, in case anyone who knew her walked by.

Dad wasn't wearing a baseball cap; he thought baseball caps looked stupid. He was wearing an old T-shirt with the words 'Little Monkeys' emblazoned on it. Underneath this title was a printed-on photo of Nat, aged four, holding a monkey in a safari park. Nat was pulling a face because the chimp had just poked her in the eye. Dad thought the picture was cute. Nat had thrown the T-shirt in the bin fourteen times. *Next time,* she thought darkly, *I'm setting fire to it. Even if Dad's wearing it.*

But even worse than the T-shirt were Dad's shorts. Dad wore shorts from June 1st to August 31st. Every year. Because, he said, "that is summer." He didn't wear them at any other time, no matter how hot, and he never wore anything else in the summer, no matter how cold or rainy. Dad was very proud of his shorts because he'd had them since he was AT SCHOOL and could still get into them. They were red and shiny and very, *very* short. Way too short. From a distance it looked like he'd just forgotten to put his trousers on. Old ladies walked past the drive, tutting and shielding their eyes.

Dad had extremely white, hairy, thin legs and in these shorts you could see almost ALL of those white, hairy, thin legs, from the ankles to the unmentionable. And when he was bending over in the van you could see a heck of a lot more and Nat could hear shrieks from the other side of the street.

To top it all, Dad had the radio on. Nat and Dad fighting over which radio station to listen to was becoming what writers of modern classics would call 'an issue'. In the old days, Nat didn't care what awful music Dad inflicted on her, because she was still finding out what music *she* liked. But now she was older and had found out what she liked – it was the music they played on RADIO ZINGG! It was happy bouncy music you could dance to. Dad liked RADIO DAD. The songs on RADIO DAD went on for hours and if you tried to dance to them you'd break your legs. They were boring and miserable and now they were playing at full blast and all the neighbours would think *she* liked

Dave Spong and his Incredible Flaming Earwigs, or whoever it was.

So Nat was very keen to get the van cleared and packed so she could hide indoors for a day or two and recover. But the more Dad chucked out onto the drive, the more stuff was still inside. It was like some evil van curse. Worse, Dad couldn't decide if the stuff he was supposed to be getting rid of would actually be useful on the trip. He kept trying to repack it.

Oh yes, the trip. *Normal families fly abroad for their holidays,* thought Nat, sourly. But Dad thought it would be 'more fun' – i.e. *cheaper* – to drive there instead.

"We'll need a car when we get there anyway," he'd argued with Mum. "And this saves us the expense of hiring one. Plus, we'll make a holiday of the journey. There's a big old tent in the van. You like camping."

This was not true. Mum hated camping. Mum liked hotels and hot water and fluffy towels and chocolates on the pillow and room service. She did not like: tents, campsites, bugs, sleeping bags, burnt sausages, shared showers, smelly loos, rain, fetching water from a pipe in a field, cows, hippies, damp socks; or any of the four great smells of camping: plastic, burnt wood, damp dirt and wee.

After a bit of shouting, Mum and Dad had come to an agreement. Or rather, Mum had made Dad agree to do what she wanted. First, Dad, Nat and Darius would take the van over to France and drive to the holiday house. Mum would then join them for a couple of weeks when Dad had found a nice hotel nearby.

"But you'll be able to stay in the house when I've done it up," argued Dad.

"I don't mean to be critical, love, but you're not a builder," Mum had pointed out. "You write jokes for Christmas crackers. I have no idea why you agreed to do this. The last time you tried to put up a bookshelf you nailed your head to a copy of *Great Expectations*."

Dad muttered something about it being a bit quiet on the Christmas cracker joke-writing job front at the moment and that it might be good for him to have another skill or two. Mum just kissed him and reminded him to take out extra health insurance and make sure the first-aid tin was full. Nat wasn't quite sure how she ended up on the bit of the trip that involved hours of van driving and staying in a falling-down house while her mum got to live it up in a hotel, but what could she do?

"Do you think we'll need this?" asked Dad, emerging backwards from the depths of the van, waving an electric pencil sharpener.

"No idea, Dad, I've got my eyes closed," shouted Nat. "Please change your shorts."

Whatever Dad said next was drowned out by the roar of a huge motorcycle engine. Oswald had arrived with Darius, who was sitting on the back of the bike. Darius hopped off and spat some flies out of his teeth. He was carrying a small tatty rucksack. It didn't look big enough to carry a decent packed lunch, let alone anything else.

"Is that all you're bringing?" asked Nat.

"It's all I've got," Darius replied lightly, before getting bowled over by the excited Dog. The two of them rolled around in the garden.

Oswald nodded to Dad, revved his motorbike and sped off without saying goodbye to his little brother.

Dad watched him go for a moment then turned back to Darius. "Best say goodbye," he said, nodding at the Dog. "We're taking him to the kennels later."

Nat was shocked. "Dad—" she began.

"I know what you're going to say," he said, cutting her off, "but he's not allowed to come with us and Mum's too busy to look after him. He'll be better off in a kennel, trust me. I've picked a nice one."

"This holiday's getting worse and worse," said Nat, running indoors. "And I think you're mean and horrible," she shouted from the hallway.

Mum was inside, on her mobile and doing emails at the same time. Nat wanted to tell her why her life was so utterly pants but didn't want to interrupt so, after hovering nearby for a few minutes, she just ran upstairs and threw herself on the bed.

Which is where she was when Bad News Nan

came looking for her a little while later.

"Your fasher said you washn't feeling very well," she said, showering Nat with biscuit crumbs. Her voice was muffled due to the addition of digestives to – and the lack of teeth in – her mouth.

Bad News Nan often kept her false teeth in her pocket so as not to wear them out by overuse. Many evenings watching TV had been livened up by the sudden discovery of Nan's gnashers under a cushion. Or in the butter dish.

"Everything's horrible," said Nat, putting her arms as far as she could round her nan.

That was music to Bad News Nan's ears. She liked nothing better than a bit of misery. "Well if you think your life's bad…" she began, and proceeded to tell Nat about:

Edna Pudding – lost two fingers in the bacon slicer at Morrison's.

Deidre Scratchnsniff – put winning lottery ticket through a hot wash.

Frank Mealtime – took a pedalo out too far at Camber Sands and was captured by Somali pirates.

His niece had to put all her bone-china figurines up on eBay to pay the ransom.

Nat wasn't too sure how true any of these were (especially the Edna story, because the last time she'd seen Mrs Pudding she was working on the checkouts not the deli counter) but funnily enough they did make her feel better.

"I've told your father this whole expedition is stupid," Nan droned on. "I said little Nat should come and stay with me this summer. Would you like that?"

Nat would like that a lot. No Dad to show her up and nothing to do except what Nan did – get up at lunchtime, watch endless episodes of *Judge Judy* and never eat a vegetable again. It sounded brilliant. Only one problem.

"How about Darius and the Dog?" Nat asked.

"I'm not looking after them," said Nan, firmly. "They'd both have to go in kennels."

Nat sighed and got off the bed. She carried on packing. France it was. But the Dog was NOT going in a kennel. She had a plan.